Mayan Civilization

A Captivating Guide to the Maya Civilization

(The True and Surprising History and Mystery of the Mayan, Religion & Gods)

Thomas Osborne

Published By **John Kembrey**

Thomas Osborne

Mayan Civilization: A Captivating Guide to the Maya Civilization (The True and Surprising History and Mystery of the Mayan, Religion & Gods)

ISBN 978-0-9952066-4-9

No part of this guidebook shall be reproduced in any form without permission in writing from the publisher except in the case of brief quotations embodied in critical articles or reviews.

Legal & Disclaimer

The information contained in this book is not designed to replace or take the place of any form of medicine or professional medical advice. The information in this book has been provided for educational & entertainment purposes only.

The information contained in this book has been compiled from sources deemed reliable, and it is accurate to the best of the Author's knowledge; however, the Author cannot guarantee its accuracy and validity and cannot be held liable for any errors or omissions. Changes are periodically made to this book. You must consult your doctor or get professional medical advice before using any of the suggested remedies, techniques, or information in this book.

Upon using the information contained in this book, you agree to hold harmless the Author from and against any damages, costs, and expenses, including any legal fees potentially resulting from the application of any of the information provided by this guide. This disclaimer applies to any damages or injury caused by the use and application, whether directly or indirectly, of any advice or information presented, whether for breach of contract, tort, negligence, personal injury, criminal intent, or under any other cause of action.

You agree to accept all risks of using the information presented inside this book. You need to consult a professional medical practitioner in order to ensure you are both able and healthy enough to participate in this program.

Table Of Contents

Chapter 1: Mayan Languages...................1

Chapter 2: Maya Writing.......................11

Chapter 3: Content Of Mayan Texts........28

Chapter 4: Literature.............................39

Chapter 5: The Earliest Mayan Literature65

Chapter 6: Izapa Civilization 75

Chapter 7: Kaminalguyu And The Mayan Highlands 86

Chapter 8: Peten And The Mayan Plains.98

Chapter 9: The Origin Of The Mayan Calendar 106

Chapter 10: Gods 116

Chapter 11: God Of Featherd Serpent ..126

Chapter 12: Mythical Creatures 150

Chapter 13: Legends 170

Chapter 1: Mayan Languages

Speakers of the Mayan languages stay very compactly. However, it ought to be stated that the Maya family includes severa cautiously associated languages but have good sized variations. A individual who speaks one of the languages of this circle of relatives will not be able to recognize a person who speaks some different language of the identical circle of relatives. It is as tough for a Maya Indian from the Yucatan to apprehend an Indian from the highlands of Chiapas as it's miles for an Englishman to apprehend a Dutchman. So some distance, it has now not been viable to unite the individual languages of this circle of relatives into sufficiently huge agencies. The reason is that for a whole lot of those languages, there isn't always a enough amount of a representative lexical base that might function the foundation for the type of systematization. Therefore, now not one of the systematizations proposed now can be considered very last.

Some college students advocate that the very first Maya had been contributors of a small Indian tribe from North America, distantly related to a number of the peoples of Southern Oregon and Northern California and further carefully associated with the Totonac and Zokway-talking Mexican peoples. Moving south, these humans began settling in western Guatemala's highlands in the center of the 1/3 millennium BC. E.

Over the subsequent millennium, the Huastecs and Yucatecs separated from the tribe. The former moved northwest and possibly settled at the territories on the coast of the Gulf of Campeche, in which the Mexican states of Tamaulipas and Veracruz are honestly located, wherein they placed themselves in reality remoted from different representatives in their ethno linguistic organisation. The Yucatecs migrated northward and spread throughout the substantial Yucatan Peninsula and the Petén plains.

The Lacandon Indians now range just a few hundred. These people, who use bows and arrows, inhabit the jungles of the Mexican u . S . Of Chiapas inside the southwestern part of the Usumacinta River basin. However, the Lacandons had been possibly an intermediate organization, no longer part of the primary tribes. In the primary half of the primary millennium BC, representatives of two greater, a good buy larger language groups, the Cholan and Tzeltal, left the authentic territory of the Maya and moved south to the essential place, in which they maintained near contacts each among themselves and with the Yucatecs dwelling to the north of them.

The similarly records of the individuals who speak the Tzeltal languages has been studied quite well in the technique of linguistic and archaeological research considering the reality that, in line with the modern records, four hundred AD. E., they have been forced to leave the great location and go back to the mountainous vicinity, settling within the mountain valleys near San Cristobal de l. A. Cases inside the Mexican united states of america of Chiapas. Representatives of other linguistic businesses which can be part of the Maya own family of languages have been plenty less willing to exchange locations. As a stop end result, their languages are greater compactly allotted. These include the archaic language of the Mam people of western Guatemala, which has only presently started to spread south to the Pacific coast, and the little-mentioned Chuh, Canjobalan, and Moto Syntlec language groups.

A type of Kiche, Kaqchikel, and associated humans of Tzutuhil, whose representatives live in villages positioned alongside the coast of Lake Atitlan, surrounded with the useful resource of using volcanoes, talk languages that a thousand years within the beyond have been a single language - Quiche. Since the time of the Spanish conquest of Mesoamerica, the Quekchi language has been dominant. It continues to gradually spread from the middle positioned in Alta Veropaz in Guatemala, taking pics the south of British Honduras and the regions around Lake Izabal in Honduras, wherein the language of the human beings changed into as soon as spoken Cheol.

So what language is the idea of Mayan writing? One examine the linguistic map is enough to look that sincerely the Yucatecs inhabit the Yucatan Peninsula. In this language, those human beings inside the northern location used Mayan hieroglyphs for writing spoke. Interestingly, the relevant a part of the linguistic map is empty. This territory has no indigenous populace besides in regions wherein the Lacandon and Kekche peoples live. But they've got lived there recently.

Not earlier than the thirteenth century. N. E., and probably masses later, a few representatives of the Yucatecs started out to move to Peten. Therefore, the hypothesis that the language of the inscriptions inside the critical vicinity turned into the language of the Yucatecs has few supporters. A few years within the past, Eric Thompson hypothesized that inside the classical length, folks who spoke the languages of the Chol group inhabited the massive place. Currently, some of them - choral and chol - inhabit the vicinity of plains and espresso hills inside the northwest, on the identical time as others - chorti - live in the southeast.

It appears indisputable that the Chol language have become as quickly as dominant within the territories alongside a large arc stretching across the complete big region. The correctness of this component of view is confirmed by way of documents concerning the time of the conquest of Mesoamerica via the Spaniards. An extra argument in pick out of this detail of view is that the language of the Mopan humans, which some researchers erroneously take a look at with the equal employer because of the reality the Yucatec language, that is, to the organization of Mayan languages right, is rather covered within the corporation of Chol languages.

It is infrequently an insignificant coincidence that the Chol language is spoken in the location wherein the ruins of the classical metropolis of Palenque are placed, and the Chorti language is spoken near Copan. The inevitable end is that the Chol-talking Maya have been the creators of all the tremendous civilizations of the essential area. However, some of the Tzeltal-speaking agencies joined them at some level in the Early Classic duration.

It is also possible that representatives of the mysterious Lacandon human beings additionally contributed to the development of these civilizations. Languages outside the Maya language circle of relatives are located in some isolated areas, indicating every a overseas invasion or remnant populations whose language has been absorbed into the Mayan languages. The little-studied Pipil people, whose representatives talk a language very close to the Nahuatl language, which changed into the dependable language of the Aztec empire, especially stay inside the west of El Salvador. Still, there are various companies of these humans on the Pacific coast and in Guatemala's valley of the Motagua River.

Some authors be given as authentic with that they invaded the Mayan territories from Mexico after the disintegrate of the

Toltec u . S . At the start of the positioned up conventional era. This concept does not contradict the records acquired in the course of the have a look at of their language using the method of lexicostatistics. The tiny organisation of Zokwe audio device who stay on the Pacific coast of the Mexican state of Chiapas and inside the border areas of Guatemala are probably traces of the as quickly as a wonderful deal wider distribution of this family of languages.

Chapter 2: Maya Writing

It is not often viable to locate any other vicinity of clinical studies wherein, with lots try expended, the effects of labor would be as stifling as even as seeking to decipher the Mayan script. The essence of the hassle isn't that we do no longer apprehend the content material of the inscriptions but that there may be a difference amongst understanding the overall which means that of the sign and the capacity to discover an equal within the Mayan language. Most success has been finished in deciphering those hieroglyphs whose meanings are associated with calendar dates or astronomy. For instance, with the aid of the use of the center of the XIX century, the French abbot Brasseur de Bourbourg, having studied the manuscript of Diego de Landa's "Reports on Affairs in the Yucatan," end up succesful, the usage of the facts cited thru this ebook, to decipher the hieroglyphs denoting the times of the Mayan calendar and successfully interpret the extensive range device, primarily based completely totally on dots and dashes, examples of which might be found inside the Maya codices. Researchers quick decided out that the Mayan texts had been written in columns, from left to proper and from top to bottom.

By the give up of the XIX century, scientists in Europe and America controlled to decipher almost all Mayan hieroglyphs related to the calendar and astronomy: signs and symptoms and signs and signs and symptoms denoting the numbers zero and 20, signs and symptoms and signs that served to designate the cardinal elements and the colours associated with them, the image for the planet Venus. It became moreover possible to decipher the hieroglyphs denoting the calendar months, the drawings of that have been given in Landa's ebook, and the "prolonged keep in mind" calendar gadget. In the early 1930s, a method to the riddle of the so-called "lunar series" have grow to be positioned because of a very a hit collaboration among astronomers and Mayan writers. But after such medical triumphs, fulfillment on this region have end up an awful lot less and plenty much less. This has led some pessimists to hypothesize, quite unreasonably, that the ones texts contained now not whatever however spells related to a cult associated with the calendar and astronomy.

Let's take as a smooth premise the notion that the Maya did have a few device of hieroglyphs used to put in writing texts no longer associated with the calendar. It appears that this shape of tool have to represent a totally confined sort of alternatives. It ought to be remembered right here that during pictographic writing systems, each signal isn't something extra than an photo of the object to which it refers - for a few primitive peoples of the place, this is sufficient. It is not viable to depict the whole lot that desires to be conveyed in photos. And as Professor Lawnsbury elements out, this is why every of the regarded writing systems, which isn't always in fact a tough and speedy of pictograms, develops in pointers - its signs gather a semantic and phonetic detail.

The development of the semantic element of the sign way that a sure image starts offevolved to particular an summary idea that doesn't have an unambiguous visible correspondence. An instance of this kind of technique is the photograph of a flame used to unique the idea of "heat". Similar standards for growing semantic meanings in hieroglyphic writing are almost everyday. The writing systems of maximum of the sector's languages that use hieroglyphics have exceeded thru similar stages of improvement. Used in its purest shape, this type of tool can be referred to as ideography, and to take a look at the records recorded with its assist, no correlation of the type of machine with any specific language is needed. Such ideographic structures encompass gadgets of mathematical symbols; as an instance, the device of Arabic numerals utilized by modern civilization, for which each of the area's languages has its names. The identical is right for the Mayan massive range tool, primarily based on the use of dots and dashes.

In its herbal shape, ideographic writing systems are hardly ever used because of the truth, due to the massive semantic load of every person, the recorded records can not be decoded unambiguously. Most people with writing systems tried to lessen ambiguity. Instead of the use of ideography, tries were made to deliver the written language systems within the course of the phonetic tool of the spoken language. The high-quality and maximum widely recognized examples of approaches this may be completed are charades and puzzles, in which ideographic symbols are used to supply the phonetic sound of a phrase or syllable. Undoubtedly, as children, every body cherished searching for to treatment such puzzles, but for people collectively with the Mixtecs and Aztecs, a writing system primarily based on such ideas became the great one they knew. But even such "charade" notation does now not exclude ambiguity. Most historic writing structures, collectively with Chinese, Sumerian, or Egyptian, are what is called "logography" - in every of those structures, the hieroglyph, which usually stands for an entire word, is the very last shape of the improvement of an ideographic or "charade" image. But an awful lot extra often, the equal hieroglyph combines each semantic and phonetic meaning and is as a result a complicated sign. One type of such signal is "charade," a phonetic photo to which a few indicator in their semantic meaning is introduced. Another type is semantic, i.E. Ideographic signs associated with phonetic symptoms and signs. Because languages have a propensity to alternate over the years, the phonetic element of the recording is regularly becoming plenty less and much less apparent, that is seen in the instance of the Chinese language. But a extra severe hassle with writing based absolutely at the logographic machine is its cumbersomeness: to learn how to examine Chinese, you want to memorize as a minimum seven thousand characters. The technique of simplification of writing always outcomes within the reality that the tool of recording the phonetic sound of a phrase starts offevolved offevolved to play an increasingly more important role. Therefore, something like a syllabic alphabet, which encompass phonetic symbols, commonly arises. Since the variety of phonemes - the smallest components that may be extremely good in sound speech - is confined in any language, the amount of characters in such an alphabet can also be restrained.

At the very last level of writing improvement, at the same time as there's a smooth separation of phonemes from each extraordinary, an alphabet arises that replaces the syllabic alphabet, typically collectively with consonant-vowel combinations. This is the very last step within the route of simplifying the writing device.

Having in brief taken into consideration the essence of the trouble, it is certainly well well worth asking the query: what device did the Maya use to document texts? Among extraordinary substances, Bishop Landa left us the famous "alphabet" with 29 characters. Several outstanding Mayan scholars have tried to use it to observe Mayan codices and one-of-a-kind texts, however they have got all failed. Some did not hesitate to announce that this "alphabet" is not anything greater than a falsification.

Researchers which might be extra cautious concept this device isn't an alphabet within the enjoy that we're aware about installing this word. For example, in Landa's "alphabet," there are as many as 3 characters denoting the sound "a", denoting the sound "b", and characters denoting the sound "l". Secondly, a number of the signs and signs are provided with remarks right now indicating that they stand for syllables, together with "ma", "ka", and "ku". We will do not forget this important circumstance a chunk later.

After all, tries to have a look at Maya texts the use of Landa's device as a actual phonetic alphabet failed almost surely. Some of the researchers rushed to the other immoderate, putting ahead that the Maya writing machine come to be in reality ideographic. However, it may have included severa "charade" signs every now and then inserted into the textual content. Thus, those pupils tried to defend the view that any of the symptoms in Mayan writing may additionally moreover need to have as many meanings and interpretations due to the fact the monks must provide you with and that first-class representatives of this caste may need to study sacred signs and symptoms and signs and symptoms, which had lots extra to do with rituals than linguistics. This factor of view can be very similar to the handiest that prevailed about the Egyptian hieroglyphs in advance than Champollion made his amazing discovery. This similarity of perspectives on the problem did no longer break out the eye of the Soviet scientist Yu.V. Knorozov, a expert in written monuments, who handled the hassle of historical Egyptian hieroglyphs. In 1952, he started out publishing a series of research wherein he another time raised the question of Diego de Landa's "alphabet" and the opportunity of Maya using elements of phonetic writing.

In the texts of the codes, in case you do not preserve in mind the diverse spellings, there are approximately 287 characters. If the Maya writing machine changed into in simple terms alphabetic, then plainly the language in which the textual content is written should have contained clearly that many phonemes. If this system had been basically syllabic, this is, syllabic, then the substantial form of phonemes can be 1/2 of. But this is not possible from a honestly linguistic issue of view. On the other hand, if all signs and symptoms and signs and symptoms of the textual content are ideograms, that is, each of the symptoms is a basically conceptual unit, inside the

Maya writing device; there have been a actually small massive variety of signs and symptoms that could not be sufficient for full verbal exchange internal a superior civilization. Taking into attention all this, Yu.V. Knorozov emerge as able to offer convincing evidence that Yu.V. Knorozov took Landa's "alphabet" due to the fact the starting point of his studies. By this time, Eric Thompson had already managed to reveal that Diego de Landa's mistake changed into that he failed to supply an explanation for to the ones from whom he received his facts exactly what he preferred, and the locals advised the bishop not the meaning of the letters and their names. If you appearance, for instance, at the number one of the sign "B" in the "alphabet", you may right now see that in its outlines, this sign resembles a footprint on the street. In the Yucatec language, the word for "avenue" looks like "bi", and that is how the letter denoting the sound "b" is called inside the Spanish alphabet. But in assessment to the Spanish language, the system of signs and symptoms and signs and symptoms applied in Maya writing isn't an alphabet however an incomplete syllabify. Knorozov come to be capable to show that the phrases drastically used within the language, sounding like a sequence of consonant - vowel - consonant (S-G-S), the Maya recorded the usage of two syllabic signs and symptoms - SG-SG, wherein the very last vowel, generally coinciding with the number one, end up now not have a look at. The proof that the Maya used exactly the phonetic, syllabic shape of writing may be the analyzing of signs, and the correctness of numerous readings carried out via Knorozov is confirmed thru using the context in which these signs and symptoms and signs and symptoms appear in the texts of the codes, in particular with the resource of the illustrations that accompany some of the passages of the textual content.

If the whole lot were restrained to this, then analyzing Mayan hieroglyphs should end up a completely easy venture, but, unluckily, there are despite the fact that numerous troubles, and the right facts of the that means of Mayan hieroglyphs additionally performs an essential function. There is pretty a whole lot of proof that phonetic factors had been frequently brought to ideographic factors to reason them to simpler to have a look at. They had been delivered both as prefixes, which indicated what the initial sound of the word become imagined to be or as postfixes, which indicated the reading of the ultimate consonant. If we are capable of decipher the this means that of these signs and symptoms, we're able to make large improvement in decoding the Mayan script. There remains lots to be finished in this area - as an instance, fine one final affirmation of the semantic and phonetic correctness of the readings of Yu.V.

It can be unfair not to mention right here the artwork of Eric Thompson and others who succeeded in decoding some extra Mayan hieroglyphs unrelated to calendar dates. Thus, it is noteworthy that the signal "ti" stated in Landa's "alphabet," according to modern studies, is a prefix that has the meanings of the preposition of the place "y," "on," and the which means that of the number one of the two signs and symptoms and signs and signs and symptoms and symptoms that Landa precise with the Latin letter "and", modified into transcribed as much like the 0.33 individual singular possessive pronoun meaning "his" or "her." Thompson turn out to be moreover able to decipher the meanings of numerous signs and symptoms and symptoms related to the magnificence of numerals, that's so crucial for the Maya language. For instance, he controlled to isolate an ideogram that corresponds to the word "te," which means "tree" or "wooded vicinity" - a sign.

Chapter 3: Content Of Mayan Texts

In all 3 Mayan codices at our disposal, there are various tables and illustrations, and, further, passages associated with the dates of the 260-day calendar are very frequently decided within the texts. None of the professionals doubts that their content cloth material is purely related to religion and astronomy. The text of these codices is a set of statements of an esoteric nature, which ought to had been study in the historic Yucatec language. The content fabric fabric of many passages of those codices probably echoes the content fabric of passages from the Chilam Balam books.

What data, then, is contained inside the Mayan inscriptions? Until these days, maximum experts believed that the content fabric material of the inscriptions did no longer fluctuate an excessive amount of from the content of books, and there has been an opinion that each one the calendar dates recorded at the monuments have been related to the life of a few form of cult in which numerous periods were deified. However, even John Lloyd Stephenson have become of a completely taken into consideration one in all a type opinion. In his notes on Copan, he wrote: "I do not forget that records is carved on his monuments. They are nevertheless looking in advance to their Champollion, who would spend the energy of his inquisitive mind on them. Who can study them?"

In 1958, Heinrich Berlin posted proof that the Maya writing machine had particular characters, the so-referred to as "brand hieroglyphs", related to some of the settlements regarded to archaeologists. Such signs are clean to differentiate for the motive that they may be usually blended with tremendous factors of hieroglyphics that seem alongside facet each. Experts have already controlled to correctly find out the "logo hieroglyphs" of eight "towns" of the classical generation: Tikal, Piedras Negras, Copan, Quirigua, Seibal, Naranjo, Palenque, and Yaxchilan. Berlin suggested that those signs and signs both denoted the names of the "towns" themselves or the dynasties that dominated in them and recommended that ancient sports were recorded at the steles and exclusive monuments of these towns.

The subsequent breakthrough on this vicinity become made with the beneficial aid of the well-known American Maya expert Tatiana Proskuryakova, who analyzed the inscriptions on 35 monuments from the "metropolis" of Piedras Negras marked with Maya calendar dates. She placed a pattern in how such monuments were placed in the front of architectural systems - all of the monuments normal seven separate corporations. Within every of those agencies, the calendar dates of the steles suit proper right into a duration that did not exceed the not unusual period of human life. Based on this, it have emerge as recommended that each organization come to be a "chronicle" of one reign. To date, there are already some data confirming this. The first monument of every business enterprise depicted a discern, most often a greater younger man, sitting in an opening above a platform or plinth. Two crucial calendar dates are typically carved in this form of steles. One of them, to which become delivered a hieroglyph in the form of an animal's head with a bandaged cheek, indicated the time whilst this character came to strength; the opposite, accompanied through a hieroglyph within the shape of a frog with legs raised, is sooner or later of the time of the beginning of this individual. Later monuments of the identical organization were possibly associated with such activities as marriages and the delivery of heirs. Proskuryakova want to pick out out signs and symptoms and symptoms and signs and symptoms associated with names and titles, in particular with the names and titles of female characters, which stand out pretty absolutely inside the sculpture of the classical Mayan technology. In addition, there are often signs of military victories on the steles, in particular if the ruler controlled to capture a few essential enemy.

Thus, the figures carved on the reliefs of the classical technology depict now not gods and monks but representatives of the ruling dynasties, their spouses, children, and topics. When the stone "chronicles" of 1 reign come to an forestall, the subsequent collection of pics begins offevolved with the same motif - the approaching to strength of a cutting-edge ruler. Perhaps the maximum entire of the "chronicles" of the guideline of the secular rulers of the historic Maya "towns" is carved on the various stone lintels of Yaxchilan. Based on the ones "files," Proskuryakova managed to reconstruct the facts of a very militant dynasty, stated via the code name "Jaguars," which dominated this metropolis in the 8th century. N. E. The records begin with a party of the exploits of a ruler named Shield-Jaguar, whose strength exceeded in 752 to someone named Jaguar-Bird, who, in all likelihood, modified into his son.

An instance of the manner masses of the content fabric of the inscriptions that accompany the reliefs carved to commemorate military victories can via now, if no longer have a study, then at least understood, can be located in lintel No. Eight from Yaxchilan, the inscription on which begins offevolved offevolved with the date "calendar circle" much like 755 AD. E. Under this calendar date is the hieroglyph "chukah," denoting, in step with the perception of Yu.V. Knorozov, the concept of "take prisoner" then comes a hieroglyph equivalent to an photograph of a skull embellished with precious stones, which, absolutely, is the name of the prisoner depicted on the proper. In the pinnacle proper nook, there are numerous greater hieroglyphs, taken into consideration one in every of this is the nominal hieroglyph of the ruler of the Jaguar Bird himself (someone with a spear), and below it's miles the "hieroglyph of the emblem" of Yaxchilan.

Of precise hobby are the ones inscriptions whose content material fabric suggests the impact exerted with the useful aid of a few "towns" on the lives of others. For instance, the "logo hieroglyph" of Yaxchilan appears on the aspect of one of the essential lady characters on the frescoes in Bonampak, and the "logo hieroglyph" of Tikal is quite not unusual on the monuments in Naranjo. Piedras Negras is positioned close to Yaxchilan, and now many experts don't forget that the well-known lintel No. Three from this city depicts the ruler of Yaxchilan "presiding" over a council that have become convened across the forestall of the 8th century. N. E., to decide who will inherit the throne in Piedras Negras.

When the trouble of Maya writing is taken into consideration, the query usually arises: why did this man or woman want to calculate the "lunar series" cycle for such epochs to date apart in time, and why did they want to feature of their calculations with dates associated with such large intervals? The solution might be associated with the fact that the rulers of the historic Mayans believed in astrology, and possibly they consulted with the priests about how the lunar cycles and the area of the heavenly our bodies are related with this or that occasion in their u.S.A., just due to the fact the Egyptians did. , Etruscans, Babylonians, and plenty of other peoples of the Old World. Astrology has its right judgment, which made no longer best the peoples of antiquity take it seriously however also human beings like Newton and Kepler. And we from time to time need accountable the Mayans for their religion.

Another place that the Mayans paid numerous interest to have come to be genealogies and troubles related to the beginning area of guy. That is why we discover dates and photos on some monuments that could handiest be associated with thoughts about who their remote ancestors had been. Berlin come to be in a characteristic to expose that the dates contained inside the inscriptions of the Temple of the Cross in Palenque may be divided into 3 agencies. The first employer consists of dates indicating a length thus far removed in time that it is able to satisfactory be related to a divine ancestor who lived in a legendary age; the second employer of dates corresponds to the remote descendants of this legendary individual who lived in not so historic instances, and, in the end, the 0.33 organization of dates is associated with current historic events.

Until now, there has now not been a person who must study the Mayan texts verbatim. Scholars are although anticipating a person who can decipher them inside the same way Champollion ought to decipher the Egyptian hieroglyphs. But it should probable be remembered that the identity of personal names and titles in Egyptian texts allowed the awesome scientist to make this discovery, and an statistics of what exactly the Mayan writing texts contained opened the way to their whole comprehension.

Chapter 4: Literature

The Mayans had books. The chronicler Ciudad Real have become cited in advance, who believed that the Mayans deserved praise for the absence of cannibalism, hobby in unnatural sexual circle of relatives participants, and the fact that they wrote books. Of course, those were now not books in our feel of the word. These had been hieroglyphic texts with illustrations. But the fact that the Maya had literature most struck the Spaniards. When the more youthful Bernal Diaz del Castillo leafed thru them within the Totonac temple at Cempoal, he noticed "numerous paper books folded in a fold... That gave me lots of meals for idea... I do not realize precisely a manner to describe it." And as we've got got visible, a number of the subjects sent to Charles V, at the facet of gold and feather adorns, had been " books of these used by the Indians." Many college students in Spain had been "astonished" at the sight of such evidence of excessive lifestyle. After all, the Maya, the Totonacs, Aztecs, Mixtecs, and almost all distinctive Indians with a evolved culture had books. However, the Maya had them for the longest time, in all likelihood eight hundred years.

During the Spanish conquest, almost each crucial middle within the Yucatan had its book depository. Even in 1697, a Spaniard said that during Tayasala (Peten), he saw statistics though made the usage of hieroglyphs.

There can be no doubt, to what extent books were used; the explanations left in this score with the beneficial useful resource of the Spaniards are noticeably wonderful. "The Indians wrote down symbols and understood every different through them." One of the critiques to the king of Spain stated: "These Ah Kines had books with icons ... And that they knew what occurred some years in the past." Diego de Landa confirms this. The Maya "knew a manner to look at and write letters, and they had symbols with which they wrote and drawings that illustrated the which means that of what changed into written ... Their books had been written on large sheets of paper, folded in folds and placed amongst forums, which they adorned; they wrote on each factors of the paper in columns, following the order of the folds. They made paper from tree roots."

Mayan paper become crafted from the internal fibers of the bark of the Ficus tree. The bark, arms huge, changed into stripped from a tree, engaging in a period of 6 m. First, it have become soaked in water to melt and extract thick white juice, and then it changed into beaten with a ribbed mallet. These moves stretched the fibers so much that a piece of bark 30 cm extensive became the paper a whole meter big. According to at least one Spaniard, the bark have become overwhelmed till it become "a sheet as thick as a Mexican actual", i.E. 2 mm. This papermaking approach is enormous; the methods, equipment for beating, and plant species associated with production are nearly the same in extensively separated regions - inside the Amazon, Africa, Polynesia, and Easter Island. In his artwork on the manufacture of paper a number of the Maya, the author of this e-book believed then that the Maya were the very first papermakers in America. Now he isn't always so tremendous. Almost all of the tribes of Central America practiced this craft, like many diverse things.

The Mayans used bark paper as clothing in advance than studying the way to weave cotton. Their monks persisted to position on clothes crafted from such paper even after the advent of weaving. The transition from garb to paper has an extended history in cultural development.

This Mayan paper (huun) have end up considerably used: manufacturing plans had been drawn on it; it end up used in fixing the labyrinths of hieroglyphs; drawings supposed for engraving on steles had been at the begin carried out to it. We recognize that the Maya had maps. Their contemporaries, the Aztecs, used amatl paper to attract up maps, and tax lists, writing chronicles and genealogies; the paper itself turned into an item of taxes.

A Spaniard who in 1697 noticed the books of the Itza Indians gave a complete and accurate account in their duration and look: from the bark of timber, they are folded like a display and painted on each aspects." The look of the 3 books which have come down to us, specifically the Dresden Codex, fits this description. It is crafted from a unmarried piece of paper received from the fibers of the bark of kopo (Ficus padiofolia). This ebook is 20 cm high, 320 cm extended, and folded like a display. Such dimensions have been given to her with the assist of heated stone irons (much like the Mexican chicaltelle), which smoothed its floor (in the Renaissance, papermakers sanded their domestic made paper with agate); in any other case it has reached its length way to a mixture of lime and starch, which offers a plant similar to cassava. Diego de Landa notes that the Maya gave their paper "a white gloss that changed into easy to put in writing down on." The paper turn out to be folded like a screen, and a ebook have become obtained. Each sheet or web web page measured approximately 7–8 via way of 20 cm. The ends of the ebook had been glued to timber boards, on which the decision of the e book turn out to be carved in hieroglyphs. The extant Codex Mexicanus has a comparable binding decorated with jade mosaics just like the jeweled bindings of Renaissance European books. The Dresden Codex has thirty-9 sheets, colored on each components and seventy-8 pages. These pages are the "rings of katuns" stated in the codex. The Mayan scribes worked with brushes crafted from the bristles of a wild pig and used dark red, mild crimson, black, blue, yellow, brown, green, and shiny black.

It is not mentioned precisely even as the Maya began to make their books. After 889 A.D. E., for unknown reasons, the Maya stopped building date-marked steles from carved stone. It turn out to be found that after that, they stored similar records on extra docile fabric like paper. It has been cautioned that throughout the twelve months 889, the number one Mayan e-book appeared.

The Dresden Codex is right of the 3 surviving Mayan books; it were given its name from the Royal Library in Dresden, which turned into added from Vienna in 1739. The true beginning area of the ebook is unknown, however its last date corresponds to 1178 AD. BC, Dr J. E. Thompson believes that this have become a new version made in the twelfth century from an actual compiled inside the early classical period (323-889). Its content material (probably, considering the reality that simplest half of of of the hieroglyphs can be deciphered) is a calendar (almanac, series) of divinations associated with girls, childbirth, and weaving. It includes tables of synodic revolutions of the planet Venus and predictions. The e-book ends with the picture of the sky god Itzamna as a celestial monster whose mouth water flows, destroying the Mayan worldwide in a flood. Of the three codices, "Dresden" - astronomical, "Tro-Cortesi - anus" - astrological, "Peresianus" - ritual. There is form of no longer something in them that may be taken into consideration statistics.

The Spaniards said that Mayan books knowledgeable about "the lives of their rulers and normal people" and "they contained a tale." 70 years after the conquest and burning of many books, a Spaniard but stated seeing books colored in specific colors, which "deliver an account in their years, tell of wars, epidemics, hurricanes, floods, famines, and one of a kind activities." Even in 1697, an Itza leader knew all about the history of the Yucatán due to the fact "he had study it in his books." It has been set up that "their hieroglyphic literature appears to have blanketed almost all branches of Maya technological knowledge," however no specimens of it have survived. The fact that the Maya treated their books because of the reality the most highly-priced shrines is validated by way of way of Landa's declaration: "The maximum valuable property that noble people took with them,

Teaching modified into the prerogative of the ruling instructions considering that "the clergymen have been the key to information ... They finished their obligations inside the temples and taught the sciences, as well as wrote books approximately them." And despite the fact that their hobby of their basis became very strong, within the ancient symbols of the Maya, it have end up now not possible to understand any private names or town names. And but we recognize that there have been coloured schemes and maps. The Popol Vuh states as a historical reality that once the Toltecs set out on their journey to the Yucatan, they "took with them their drawings, wherein everything end up written down concerning historical times" and that the Maya from the mountains acquired from the cibals tulan, drawings from historic Tula (the remaining capital of the Toltecs), "with which they recorded their information". The similarity between some homes in Chichen Itza and Tula (Tollan), placed

745.Sixty five mi from every distinct, is so precise that architectural statistics may be conveyed in no distinctive manner than via drawings made on paper. In addition, the Maya had books on remedy, copies made inside the 18th century, and written in Latin letters, which had been no question first translated from hieroglyphs into the written language of the Maya. José de Acosta, who traveled appreciably in Peru and Mexico (1565), wrote: "There have been books in which Indian pupils saved ... Their know-how of flora, animals and various things." Nevertheless, they did no longer use their hieroglyphic script to put in writing contracts - "there were no written agreements in the sale and purchase" - and this grow to be a supply of false impression and warfare of terms, which frequently introduced about warfare.

In addition, the Mayans had books on remedy, copies made in the 18th century, and written in Latin letters, which were no question first translated from hieroglyphs into the written language of the Maya. José de Acosta, who traveled considerably in Peru and Mexico (1565), wrote: "There have been books in which Indian scholars saved ... Their knowledge of plants, animals and super topics." But they did not use their hieroglyphic script to write down contracts - "there had been no written agreements within the sale and buy" - and this modified into a supply of false impression and conflict of phrases, which regularly caused conflict. In addition, the Maya had books on remedy, copies made inside the 18th century, and written in Latin letters, which had been no question first translated from hieroglyphs into the written language of the Maya. José de Acosta, who traveled substantially in Peru and Mexico (1565), said: "There were books in which Indian scholars stored ... Their expertise of plants, animals and extraordinary matters." But they did now not use their hieroglyphic script to put in writing contracts - "there had been no written agreements within the sale and purchase" - and this modified right into a deliver of false impression and battle of phrases, which regularly added approximately struggle. "There had been books in which Indian pupils saved ... Their information of plants, animals and different matters." But they did now not use their hieroglyphic script to install writing contracts - "there have been no written agreements within the sale and buy" - and this modified proper right into a supply of confusion and war of phrases, which frequently caused conflict. "There have been books wherein Indian college students saved ... Their facts of flowers, animals and various things." But they did no longer use their hieroglyphic script to jot down down contracts - "there have been no written agreements inside the sale and buy" - and this end up a source of confusion and disagreement, which often added approximately struggle.

The Aztecs, whose writing have become loads a great deal much less evolved than the Mayans, stored accurate information of the amount and first rate of tribute and profits and had maps of possessions and an extensive map of Tenochtitlan. We apprehend the right series in their rulers and the names of all the historical cities and provinces of the Aztecs. (The Aztecs moreover left in the back of great literature, which became positioned on paper through Spanish-Aztec scribes within the 16th century.) As for the Mayans, we failed to even recognize the names in their "kings" till presently. Even the Incas, who did not have a written language, had a quipu knot script (after 1250); it acted as a mnemonic that gave them—and now us—the chronology in their data. Perhaps the Mayan hieroglyphic script is not a written language in any respect but greater of a mnemonic system, way to which the reader's reminiscence was awakened with the pics of the gods, dates, and symbols. This question arises because of the fact that that they had rhythmic songs. The historic Greeks, led thru the goddess of reminiscence Mnemosyne, sang, commencing the historic occasions of the past clothed in length. The Iliad became chanted long in advance than Homer wrote it down. The Druids used bards to report their past occasions and treatises on geography, the ocean, and agricultural practices in mnemonic rhythm. Henry III (1207-1272, King of England 1216-1272 - Ed.) used the versification Regis to sing rhymed chronicles, epitaphs, and so forth. Led via manner of the goddess of memory, Mnemosyne, they sang, starting up the historical sports of the past clothed in length. The Iliad became chanted lengthy earlier than Homer wrote it down. The Druids used bards to document their past sports and treatises on geography, the sea, and agricultural practices in mnemonic rhythm. Henry III (1207-1272, King of England 1216-1272 - Ed.) used the versification Regis to sing rhymed chronicles, epitaphs, and the likes led with the aid of the goddess of memory Mnemosyne. They sang, starting up the historical sports of the past clothed in period. The Iliad turn out to be chanted extended before Homer wrote it down.

The Druids used bards to file their past events and treatises on geography, the sea, and agricultural practices in mnemonic rhythm. Henry III (1207-1272, King of England 1216-1272 - Ed.) used the versification Regis to sing rhymed chronicles, epitaphs, and so on. English king in 1216-1272. - Ed.) used versification Regis to sing rhymed chronicles, epitaphs, and so on. English king in 1216-1272. - Ed.) used versification Regis to sing rhymed chronicles, epitaphs, and so forth.

But if the Mayan books included areas other than those the surviving codices added to us, we would in no way recognize approximately it because of the reality the Spanish clergymen destroyed them. Diego de Landa says bluntly: "... We burned they all ..."

It turned into ordered: idolatry to be eliminated. Diego de Landa himself signed this decree in 1562. As a part of the Spanish spiritual software, all Maya books had been captured and brought to the town of Mani. "We discovered a big amount of books," Landa wrote, "and there has been now not whatever in them that did no longer show superstition and devilish lies, so we burned all of them, which they [the Maya] regretted and grieved about amazingly." This is showed with the aid of the historian's get right of entry to from 1633. In Mani Landa "collected the books and ordered them to be burned. They burned many ancient books about the records of the Yucatan, which told about its origins and statistics and which have become of such terrific fee. José de Acosta that located Jesuit who traveled through Peru and Mexico inside the younger people of this worldwide have become enraged through such iconoclastic efforts: "It follows from a few silly zeal even as,

Diego de Landa did this art work with enough care; out of loads of books, best three escaped this mass destruction.

The good sized content material of the Mayan texts is understood. Even scientists with complete statistics doubt that statistics of ancient events were made on monuments. Here is a trendy example of a Mayan text located on stele in Tikal, included with terrific carvings: "5 Ahau thirteen Muan; the finishing touch of the depend of fourteen, the very last touch of the tun. The access is related to the calendar. There isn't any factor out of the name of the metropolis, the call of the ruler, or any historic events that came about in the course of "6 Ahau 13

Muan". The inscriptions made on awesome Maya monuments in awesome places are of the same kind.

How one of a type from those kind of information within the Middle East! They are tautological, verbose , and informative, which encompass "The Sixty-Two Curses of Esarhaddon." By Mayan standards, this Assyrian-talking pill is pretty tiny (forty five with the useful resource of 30 cm). It does now not range masses in fashion from the Palenque capsules: the god-kings hurl thunder and lightning at their kneeling vassals. In May 672 B.C., the Assyrian king Esarhaddon swore allegiance to his vassals and referred to as on them to terrible curses if they violated it. He demanded that his son Ashurbanipal turn out to be his successor. This tablet exudes emotion; the names themselves sound similar to the roar of cymbals: "...

And allow Sarantius, who offers light and seed, wreck your names and land ... Allow Ishtar, the goddess of wars and battles (further to fertility, sensual love, and plenty of others. - Ed.), weigh down your bows ... " So, till all sixty- curses were spoken. This tablet offers us dates, facts, human beings, and characters.

What can you look at the Mayans from their hieroglyphic texts like this?

"Katun eleven Ahau is prepared on a mat, set on a throne. When the ruler reigned: Ishkal Chak sat going through their ruler.

The heavenly fan will descend; heaven's gate, heaven's bouquet will descend.

The drum of Lord 11 Ahau will sound another time; his rattle will sound yet again.

When the flint knives are located into his robe, that day may be inexperienced turkey, that day might be Sulim Chan, and that day could be Chakanputun.

They will find out their harvest most of the wooden and the numerous rocks, those who misplaced their harvest inside the Katun of Lord eleven Ahau."

Texts of this kind are determined inside the route of the Mayan u.S.A. Of the united states.

It rarely occurs that they have got some element else besides this nearly pathological preoccupation with time. The years have been a burden carried through the gods, correct or evil, however now not unbiased. Appropriate rituals have to influence terrible gods, and there was "an opportunity to ease Ish's grief and follow balm to Kauak's woes.» Like us, the Maya judged human actions through the ache and satisfaction they introduced about. What have become carved on the Mayan monuments became intended to steer the gods, but it grow to be from time to time a few thing from literature in our facts.

In addition to the three surviving Maya codices and the large fashion of hieroglyphic texts on monuments, we've the Books of Chilam-Balam (Books of the Jaguar Priest). The Mayan textual content is written in Latin letters. The dates of the composition range most of the number one 1/2 of of the 16th century, whilst the Mayan conquest changed into a fait accompli, and the surrender of the 18th century. Their problems are just like the contents of what changed into deciphered within the Mayan books. Maya clergymen dictated texts from books that had escaped burning to a bilingual scribe who wrote the Mayan language in Latin characters. These books aren't chronicles in our feel. However, if they are literature, then permit those books talk for themselves. The first traces of considered considered one of them observe:

"This is the order of the Katuns because of the reality [itsa] left their u . S . A ., their domestic in Nonowal.

Four Katuns remained tutul shiu, Ahau-10 Ahau, [849–928] at the decline of the Tsuyu people."

These books speak lots approximately the «Tsuyu language," a kabbalistic (cryptic) shape of language utilized by monks to grow to be privy to their type and whether or not or now not they knew the statistics of the rites. You can see how the textual content is meant for voice. This shows that plenty of Mayan literature became oral, like exceptional historic cultures.

Mayan literature become symbolic and precis. It grow to be antisocial; great the initiated must understand the which means and importance of its symbols. Yet, what can we have at the same time as the characters are translated? The Mayans say no longer whatever approximately themselves or their facts. A smooth date is intangible; it lacks blood and ardour if associated with good sized activities in people's lives. Time knows its business enterprise. Everything precis and symbolic in literature disappears and dissolves into skinny air. Everything honestly packed with sounds disappears with the wind.

Chapter 5: The Earliest Mayan Literature

The historical Mayan epic story "Popol Vuh" tells how the gods-forefathers Tepeu and Gukumatz raised the earth from the abyss of water and populated it with animals and plants. Having performed this, the divine ancestors longed for reverence and admiration and molded human-like beings out of the earth, but they became out to be quick-lived and modified into dust yet again after some time. The gods created the subsequent race from wood; however the advent grew to come to be out to be so brainless that the gods, who changed it with people made from meat, destroyed it. However, those creatures became to evil and were destroyed at the same time because the gods added down a horrible downpour on the planet:

a big flood swept them off the face of the earth.

Finally, from corn dough, the gods created actual people, the ancestors of the Maya Quiche. Neither the traditions of the Indians nor archaeological research can shed moderate at the beginning of the Mayans. The individuals who live in a tribal tool do not keep ancient reminiscence for prolonged, and the complex geological situations of this region, combined with lush plants, make it very hard to find the remains of the material lifestyle of historical times.

There are few herbal caves and rock formations in this place that could feature a habitat for primitive hunters and gatherers. In this area, specifically within the tropical rainforest region, it's far very hard to discover places in which open regions are positioned.

We can simplest wager whilst someone regarded within the territories in which the Mayan civilization ultimately arose. The first to populate the New World had been immigrants from Asia who moved to America sooner or later of the ice age on the prevent of the Pleistocene, at the identical time as a bridge but existed on the internet site on-line of the cutting-edge Bering Strait.

Even earlier than the begin of the 9th millennium BC. E. The first Indians set up their camps at the beaches of the windswept Strait of Magellan. It may be assumed that with the resource of this time, primitive hunters had already settled on the territory of each Americas. Large expanses of every continents have been then included with grass, on which massive herds of herbivores roamed - mammoths, horses, camels, and large bison. In the usa, Canada, and Alaska, wherein severa web sites relationship decrease again to the most ancient generation had been decided, this early lifestyle, known as "clovis" and has not but observed out all its secrets and techniques and techniques and techniques to archaeologists, existed for approximately 10-12 thousand years again.

The crucial way of incomes a livelihood for the humans of the Clovis era turned into looking for mammoths. Scientists concluded by using the use of manner of analyzing the remains in locations in which the ones animals were as quickly as hunted - inside the southwest of America. Huge elephants had been killed with darts for throwing, and there had been special devices. The darts were equipped with superbly made stone elements, which the researchers call grooved due to the truth grooves resemble scales from their base on one or each additives. Such suggestions are located within the north of Alaska, Nova Scotia and in the regions of Mexico and Central America, masses to the south. They have even been positioned in Costa Rica and Panama.

The oldest synthetic object observed in Maya territory is a small obsidian tip for a throwing weapon, spear, or dart near San Rafael. Its belonging to the Clovis way of life can be decided with the useful resource of the grooved floor on one of the components and with the beneficial aid of the truth that the rims of the cease are chipped on the factor of attachment to the shaft. This point strongly resembles severa others located in Mexico, and smaller factors from the Clovis life-style, have been observed inside the United States. These few unearths quality advocate that on the surrender of the ice age, primitive hunters roamed the excessive mountain location of the Maya.

The Rise of the Mayan Civilization

Several conflicting hypotheses have already been suggest concerning the emergence of the Mayan civilization. One of the most odious ideals is that the previously unremarkable Mayan Indians fell underneath the have an impact on of tourists who came to them from the seashores of China. Here we should make a digression and clarify for non-experts, which can be categorically stated - not one of the subjects determined inside the Mayan cultural centers has been recognized as an object from the Old World and due to the fact the time of Stephenson and Cather timber, theories of transatlantic or transpacific contacts with careful medical interest commonly crumbled. Followers of each different scientific direction, based at the supposedly low agricultural capability of Peten and Yucatan, argue that

Another hypothesis shows that the rural capability of those regions is greatly underestimated and the Maya life-style, as it's far identified to us from the classical length, is absolutely sui significant (Original (lat.)), bearing no traces of outside have an effect on. It must be stated that each the ones factors of view are exaggerated and at the least in element faulty. The fact is that the Maya of every the highlands and the plains were in no way isolated from the relaxation of Mesoamerica, and, as we're capable of see on this and next chapters, in the course of their data, beginning from the maximum ancient instances, the Mayan tradition end up inspired by means of using cultures that existed in what's now Mexico.

What exactly can we suggest thru the word "civilization?" How exactly is civilization particular from savagery? Archaeologists typically strive to influence clean of this sort of query, and as opposed to a formulated solution, they provide a whole listing of abilties that they agree with are inherent in civilization. One of the essential requirements is taken into consideration to be the presence of towns, but, as we will speedy see, neither the Maya of the classical duration nor numerous other historical civilizations had some issue similar to what we used to outline the idea of "city," each other essential criterion of civilization is the presence of a written language. But the Incas of Peru, who created a complex civilization, were illiterate.

Civilization differs from what preceded it in quantitative in choice to qualitative phrases. However, in fact, no civilization can rise up in advance than the establishments of the u . S ., temples, big public works, and substantial, unified creative patterns... With few exceptions, there may be a want for a complex country gadget to keep information in a few form, and writing generally arises in reaction to this need. More or a good deal much less correct processes of maintaining time are generally created for the equal purpose.

It must not be forgotten that, no matter commonplace features, each of the civilizations is unique in its manner. The Mayans of the classical period, who lived in a mountainous region, had an complex calendar, writing, pyramidal temples, and palaces constructed of limestone blocks; internal were rooms with vaulted ceilings. They additionally had a manner of existence of architectural making plans, even as a few homes in the course of the market rectangular have been distinguished thru numerous rows of stone steles in the the front of them.

In addition, that they had polychrome ceramics and a complex inventive fashion, which manifested itself in every bas-reliefs and wall artwork. All those feature abilities of the classical length are simply absent in the substances discovered up to now regarding the past due archaic (3 hundred BC - a hundred and fifty AD) and preclassical (one hundred fifty-three hundred AD) periods.

Chapter 6: Izapa Civilization

The most important supply of facts needed to find out the essential element to fixing the thriller of the manner the highly advanced Mayan civilization arose exemplify the cloth remains of the Hispanic civilization. The excessive hobby in the entirety connected with this way of life is described through the fact that she, each in time and in vicinity, occupies an intermediate feature some of the Olmec way of life of the Middle Archaic length and the early classical Mayan way of life. Monuments bearing the imprint of the uncommon artistic fashion of this way of lifestyles are scattered over a huge territory stretching from Tres Zapotes, mendacity on the Atlantic coast of the dominion of Veracruz, to the plains of Chiapas and Guatemala, located on the Pacific coast, and further, as a good buy because the city of Guatemala.

During its heyday, Izapa have become a top religious and cultural middle, in which more than eighty temple foundations have survived to in the mean time - pyramidal mounds covered with river stones. This settlement is placed inside the low hills east of Tapachula, Chiapas, in an area with a wet climate 20 miles from the Pacific coast.

The question of whether or not or now not to recall this agreement one of the cultural and spiritual centers of the Maya or to function it to one of the cultures of pre-Hispanic Mexico has now not but been resolved, but the language spoken right right here in antiquity turn out to be now not one of the Mayan languages, but the tapachulteco language, an extinct language belonging to the Zokwean employer, whose languages were as quickly as hundreds greater vast than they may be now. Even even though

Izapa became founded as a spiritual center relationship lower returned to the early Archaic length, and lasted until the Early Classic duration, maximum of its architectural systems and all huge sculptures belong to the Late Archaic to Preclassic durations.

The maximum function of Izapa's creative fashion is the big, ambitious, but mainly ornate scenes that seem in most of the carvings of this lifestyle. The plots of the numerous pics are secular, which include the photo of a person in a splendid in shape decapitating a defeated enemy. Still, there are also plots with non secular topics. Among the latter, the most commonplace is the picture of a deity called the "extended-lipped god." It emerge as depicted with an exorbitantly elongated better lip and fireside escaping from the nostrils. This character actually represents a in addition improvement of the photograph of the Olmec werewolf jaguar, the god of rain and lightning.

Certain habitual icons are, in all likelihood, factors of traditional iconography. These embody a signal harking back to the Latin letter U, positioned among slashes, which turned into normally placed above the precept level and may were an early model of the sky band signal, so brilliant in classical Maya paintings. The "U" signal itself is maximum probable the prototype of any other hieroglyph for the moon, and it could arise numerous instances in a single bas-comfort.

The famous belonging to the Hispanic culture have many skills feature of the heyday of the civilization of the Mayan plains, together with stele-altar complexes and the "long-lipped god," whose photograph is already beginning to convert into the rain god Chaka. They furthermore embody the imaginitive style of carvings on bas-reliefs, gravitating in the direction of depicting historic and mythological scenes, wherein particular hobby turn out to be paid to a headdress adorned with feathers and different information of the dress. There is not any writing or calendar, however on the slopes of the mountain levels stretching eastward along the Pacific Ocean to Guatemala, there are monuments with inscriptions and calendar dates relationship lower lower back to the Baktun 7 length.

One such place in Guatemala is Abah-Takalik, placed south of Colombo, inside the foothills covered with lush flowers and abundant in moisture, which ultimately of the time of the Conquest end up well-known for growing cocoa beans. Coffee is now the number one crop grown on this region. In look, Abah-Takalik resembles Isapa - mounded hills scattered in disorder all through the territory of the agreement. Less than a mile from the relevant organization of mounded foundations is a huge boulder carved in pure Olmec fashion with the photograph of a bearded had been-jaguar. From this, we are in a role to complete that the Olmecs as soon as visited this territory.

Stela 1 from Abah-Takalik is handiest Hispanic in style but isn't dated. On the alternative hand, at the pretty broken Stele 2, there may be a bas-treatment depiction of Hispanic characters in fantastic costumes and excessive headdresses adorned with feathers dealing with every certainly one of a type. Between them does a vertical row of hieroglyphic signs, and under, from carved curls resemble a cloud, the face of the god of heaven peeps out? The first, uppermost character in the column of hieroglyphs is truely the earliest form of the "introductory hieroglyph." which appears inside the later classical Mayan texts on the start of the Long Count calendar dates. Directly underneath, it's far the numerical coefficient of Baktun, which honestly manner the variety 7.

Stela 1 from Izapa on displayNational Museum of Anthropology, Mexico City

A excellent Baktun-era hieroglyphic inscription 7 is positioned on stele 1, or Guererra stele, from El Baul, that is positioned southeast of Abah-Takalik, amongst coffee plantations, in an area of properly-researched centers of the Kotsumalhuapa manner of life dating once more to the Early Classic duration.

Since its discovery in 1932, heated debates have flared up spherical this item. It is concept that the starting region of this item dates lower returned to a time later than the classical era. On the proper side of this stele is depicted a parent of a person have come to be in profile in a disturbing pose with a spear in his hand. Above the top of the parent is a bandage hides a cloud-like cluster of curls, the decrease part of the face, and the headdress has ribbons tied under the chin, a detail widely known in Maya art work of the plains thinking about that historic instances. There are columns of carved signs and symptoms and signs and symptoms within the the the front of the determine. The proper one consists of flat oval pills, which had to be signed with paints.

The icons positioned in the left vertical row deserve extra interest. They constitute the primary calendar date on a monument inside the Maya vicinity. At the top of this column is the icon for the numerical factor 12, right now underneath, an element formed like a skeletal jaw, the sign observed in Mexican cultures for the day of Eb. Then there are four indecipherable characters, placed via a series of icons indicating the numerical coefficients of the "prolonged depend" tool, which, deliberating the connection with the day Eb of the "calendar circle", can be look at as 7.19.15.7.12. According to our reckoning, this corresponds to 36 A D, that is, this calendar get right of access to refers to a date this is 256 years earlier than every other date,

Before thinking about the regions of the Pacific coast, one extra stylistic direction of huge sculpture want to be stated, that is big each in those territories and in

Kaminalguya. The expression of this style is large, as an possibility primitive statues depicting human beings with cauldron-like bellies, puffy faces, and decrease jaws so protruding that they have been in evaluation to Mussolini's past due images. Near the agreement of Monte Alto, located near El Baul, there may be a whole enterprise of such monsters positioned in a row. There is also a big stone head made in the identical fashion. This sculptural complex is thought to be related to the Olmec manner of lifestyles, which preceded the Hispanic. However, for the reason that entire territory of Monte Alto is strewn with clay shards related to the overdue archaic duration, this kind of hypothesis seems debatable. Rather, it may be assumed that these statues are related to one of the minor religious cults that existed concurrently with the cult of the

Hispanic rain god, virtually as the religions and innovative forms of the Greco-Roman and Egyptian civilizations coexisted and flourished in historical Alexandria.

But to which god come to be this cult dedicated? This deity should nice be a "fat god," whose cult turn out to be big the numerous peoples who inhabited Mexico and the northern Mayan vicinity in the classical generation. However, we do now not recognise a few factor approximately the capabilities that he completed.

Chapter 7: Kaminalguyu And The Mayan Highlands

The late archaic period noticed the flourishing of the Miraflores way of existence. At that point, Kaminalguyu, a number one cultural and spiritual center, the remains of which may be although preserved at the western outskirts of Guatemala, turned into Izapa's rival inside the beauty of monumental sculpture in duration and some of bulk temple foundations. People who lived inside the remaining centuries CE constructed maximum of the 2 hundred temple foundations observed, at some point of the Miraflores diploma. The Kaminalguyu rulers at that factor in all likelihood wielded outstanding economic and political strength, which extended over an entire lot of the Maya mountain region. The excavations of burials belonging to the "Miraflores" degree brought many find out testifying to the pricey they used to surround themselves with. Bulk hill for the amount E-III-3, positioned close to Kaminalguyu, consists of numerous temple systems, every of which modified into constructed on top of the preceding one and modified right into a stepped pyramid with a flat pinnacle, at the the the front aspect of which there was a enormous staircase. The very last pinnacle of the embankment is over 60 toes. Since the ancient builders did now not have without issues processed stone, ordinary clay, baskets with earth, and family rubbish served as constructing substances for the pyramid's production.

The temples were houses with thatched roofs supported thru vertical wooden helps. Each time they had been buried, they had been rebuilt. The grave, the development of which started out from the top of the mound, grow to be a chain of successively reducing square recesses, going deeper and deeper into the pyramid, into the layers of the previous temple structures. After the give up of all the ceremonies, the burial modified into immured under a ultra-modern clay floor. Pyramids served as burial internet sites till the classical technology. The deceased's frame have become wearing a notable outfit and protected with pink paint from head to toe; then, they placed him on a timber stretcher and faded him into the grave. The our bodies of sacrificed adults and youngsters had been additionally located there, rich offerings, the abundance of that is sudden. Over 300 incredible products have been in one of the graves; some of them had been positioned subsequent to the frame of the buried, others - on its timber ceiling. Ancient grave robbers, who entered through an opening common due to the destruction of one of the burials mendacity deep inside the pyramid, stole jade jewelry from the burial internet website on line.

Among the burial garments observed within the grave have been the remains of a masks or headdress composed of jade plates, which had been probable as soon as related to a wooden base, jade rings, a bowl carved from crystalline schist, at the ground of which can be engraved ordinary for the "Miraflores" level scroll styles, small carved bottles made from fuchsite and soapstone.

Although the ceramic vessels of the Miraflores degree, placed both inside the E-Sh-three burial and a few exclusive locations, are made inside the conventional way, which changed into not unusual within the Late Archaic period subsequently of southeastern Mesoamerica from Izapa to El Salvador and beyond, as a whole lot as the great and northern areas of the Maya, they'll be very distinct from the rest of the ceramics in their sophistication.

The shape of the vessels turns into greater complicated, as their contours collect curved outlines, the floor is decorated with decorative elements, and vessels on legs seem. Sometimes they were made in the shape of humorous collectible figurines. Some of them depict a smiling old guy. Painted gypsum changed into used for the red and inexperienced colors to seem on the floor of ceramic merchandise after firing. Most of the bowls and jugs are adorned with scroll carvings. In manufacturing "usulutan" ceramics, an uncommon approach of decorative decoration of the product become used an indicator of the late archaic duration. It is thought that such ceramics first seemed on the territory of El Salvador, wherein they won huge popularity. On the ground of these merchandise, which have been in superb call for optimum of the Maya, a layer of shielding substance, which incorporates wax or a thin layer of clay end up carried out with a flat brush. After that, the products were darkened over low warmth, exposing them to smoke. Then the protective cloth grow to be eliminated, and on the product's floor, there has been a sample of parallel wavy traces of yellowish colour on a dark orange or brown history.

At one time, there was an opinion that people of the Miraflores diploma made best the so-referred to as "mushroom-formed stones" from stone sculptures. The cause of these precise gadgets, considered considered one of which changed into determined in E-Sh-three, is dubious. Some recall they may be primitive phallic symbols. Others, together with Dr Borhegi, accomplice them with the cult of hallucinogenic mushrooms, which stays common within the mountainous regions of Mexico. Proponents of this idea insist that the mortars and pestles often located with those stone objects have been used for rituals concerning the training of medicine.

Since the Kaminalguyu hills were subjected to barbaric destruction at a few diploma within the production of latest city blocks, a huge type of substances grew to come to be out to be on the floor, allowing us to take a glowing have a have a observe what passed off in this period. It became out that in the time of the Miraflores way of lifestyles, there were artists who should create big sculptural works in stone inside the Hispanic innovative fashion, that is the forerunner of the classical Mayan style. Moreover, representatives of the elite agencies of the Kaminalguyu population knew the way to write down at a time on the same time as the relaxation of the Maya humans had been simply starting to realize what writing have become.

Two such monuments have been discovered on the same time as laying a drainage trench. The first is a granite stele depicting a strolling guy who's sporting numerous masks of the Hispanic "prolonged-lipped god" right away. On the only hand, this character contains a rather intricate flint item. On both facet of it are burning clay censers, just like the ones decided within the course of excavations of layers with Miraflores ceramics.

Another stele is even greater unusual. Before it modified into deliberately damaged into portions, it may have been splendid and, judging by way of the surviving fragments, modified into embellished with pics of severa Hispanic gods. Bearded, certainly one of them ties a individual with tridents have come to be with their factors down as opposed to eyes. He is probably the forerunner of some of the gods that later seemed in Tikal. The hieroglyphs carved close to the ones figures may be their calendar names considering that, in historic Mesoamerica, every gods and people were diagnosed with the times of the calendar on which they were born. The longer textual content, which incorporates severa columns of hieroglyphs, is written in a script that has not but been observe. According to severa pupils, it could be considered the forerunner of classical Mayan writing considering that it's far very just like it in shape.

Skilled artisans of the Miraflores manner of existence made no longer most effective big-sized steles. Among the reveals, there also are carved figures of frogs and toads of numerous sizes, known as silhouette sculptures, which possibly need to have been set up vertically internal temples or in squares the use of spike fastening.

The often encountered pix of a person already acquainted to us with a big, bowler-like stomach belong to the identical period. On this event, the query yet again arises: are these figures, not sacred gadgets of worship, commonplace among normal humans whose beliefs differed clearly from the aristocratic faith in their rulers? But the ones researchers who bear in mind the ones objects to belong to unique cultural layers may be proper.

The brilliant richness of the fabric subculture of the "Miraflores" diploma, the perfection of its architectural and innovative creations, and the apparent connection with classical Mayan art, manifested inside the creative fashion, pictorial plots, and writing gadget - all this lets in us to finish that the Hispanic lifestyle of the mountainous region notably stimulated the formation of a particularly evolved civilization of the essential and northern regions of the Maya.

But, irrespective of all of the successes that the Kaminalguyu civilization completed throughout the overdue archaic period, via the second century. N. E., its famous person started out to set, and after a century or , there has been not something left of it but ruins. Only in the early classical duration, at the identical time as there was a high invasion of the tribes from the territory of Mexico, this place regained its former beauty.

Chapter 8: Peten And The Mayan Plains

At the same time that the past due archaic culture flourished in the Mayan mountains and at the Pacific coast, the essential and northerly areas additionally skilled a fast upward thrust. Temples of big non secular and cultural facilities towered above the areas cleared inside the jungle. But the way of life of the Mayans, who lived inside the plains, advanced in a one in all a kind route from their kindred peoples of the southern territories. They speedy started to address the ones unique features that high-quality them in the classical length.

At that point, in the northern and essential Mayan areas, the primary characteristic belonged to the Chikanel manner of existence, which, notwithstanding the difference in its factors in great areas, grow to be particularly homogeneous. As well as within the southern vicinity, the function talents of this era are "usulutan" ceramics and exceptional-necked vessels adorned with carefully sculpted rims. Monochrome merchandise predominate - red or black, with a waxy surface to touch. There are nearly no vessels at the legs. It seems as an opportunity everyday that no figurines were decided in the most famous cultural and spiritual centers of the "Chikanel" culture. This suggests that some changes have taken place in spiritual cults.

Clay vessel with a image

sacred chicken quetzal

Bowl in the fashion of ceramics usulutan

However, the most important distinguishing feature of the Chikanel degree is the immoderate, in particular on the stop of the Late Formative degree (a hundred BC - a hundred fifty AD), stage of structure improvement. It have to be recalled that, from a geological thing of view, the territory of Petén-Yucatan has massive reserves of effects processed limestone, and right right here flint is determined in abundance, from which equipment may be made. Moreover, even at some point of the Mammon level, the Mayans of the plain quarter decided that in case you burn portions of limestone and mix the following powder with water, you get a white lime mortar that firmly holds the stones collectively. Finally, they speedy determined that they will use filler made from limestone chips and clay, a form of historic concrete in advent.

Therefore, even in historical instances, Mayan architects should collect their temples, growing real architectural masterpieces. Excavations on this vicinity's biggest Mayan cultural and spiritual centers - Vashaktuna and Tikal - showed that already on the prevent of the Chikanel diploma, their vital pyramids, temple structures, and ritual internet websites commenced out to take their very last form. It is commonly familiar, as an instance, that the E-VII-sub temple platform at Washaktun changed into built on the stop of the chikanel diploma. Perfectly preserved below the modern strata, this platform - a pyramid with a truncated pinnacle - is included on top with a layer of white plaster and includes several ranges, every of which has a bulk threshold - a completely feature characteristic of the shape of the Mayan plains. In the middle of every facet of the pyramid is a staircase buried in its floor, adorned on the rims with masks of huge monsters, wherein a few researchers see the transformed image of the Olmec god of rain. However, some of them are in all likelihood photos of a heavenly serpent. Holes made at the floor for polls suggest that at the higher platform of the pyramid, there has been a building built of poles or reeds.

Just a few hours' stroll south of Washaktun, is some other most crucial center of Maya lifestyle - Tikal. His temples are in no manner inferior of their architectural perfection and possibly even surpass those of Vashaktun. At the top of the houses belonging to the late duration of the "Chikanel" level, there have been spiritual buildings, of which most effective partitions product of stone have survived, and it's miles quite viable to count on that their rooms were blanketed with a stepped, or, as it's also referred to as, "fake" vault... The walls of this type of temples are embellished on the outdoor with a instead unusual painting depicting human figures fame closer to a information of cloud-like curls. The hand of an expert artist who used black, yellow, red, and pink paints for this artwork genuinely makes it. Another piece of wall painting, this time painted in black paint on a purple records, end up positioned at Tikal internal a burial furthermore from the late Chikanel length. It depicts six characters in outstanding costumes, amongst which, likely, there are every human beings and gods. These works probably belong to the second one half of of the first c. BC e., made in an genuinely Hispanic fashion, very just like that commonplace in Kaminalguya.

Some of the burials of Tikal, belonging to the overdue archaic period, display that the ruling elite of the "Chikanel" diploma in terms of role in society and wealth emerge as in no manner now not as first-rate because the representatives of the top strata of society of the "Miraflores" level. An example is Burial eighty five, positioned at the base of the temple platform, like every particular burials of this period. Only one skeleton changed into determined inside the burial chamber blanketed with a primitive stepped vault. It seems unexpected that this skeleton lacks a cranium and femurs. Still, given the richness and form of devices located on this burial, it may be assumed that this man died at some point of the conflict. His topics later determined his frame, mutilated via enemies. The stays were smartly wrapped in cloth and stored in an upright role. A small masks of green stone, with eyes and tooth fabricated from mother-of-pearl, related to the top of this package deal deal, was imagined to update the missing head.

In addition to its terrifying contents, the bundle deal additionally contained a thorn and the lower again plate of a sea urchin, a creature the Maya considered a picture of self-sacrifice. Near the burial chamber, specially hiding places, at the least 26 vessels had been located courting once more to the surrender of the "Chikanel" degree; in considered without a doubt certainly one of them, charred portions of pinewood were observed, which, in line with radiocarbon assessment, belong to the period from the sixteenth to 131 CE e.

Remains of the beyond beauty of the fabric way of lifestyles of the Late Archaic duration are placed inside the Maya flat location, everywhere the archaeologist's shovel plunges into the deep layers of the soil. Even within the northern vicinity, that is tons much much less rich in archaeological well-known, there are monuments of amazing shape of this era, collectively with the big artificial hill of Uaksuna - a temple platform, the bottom of it's a rectangle measuring 60 through the use of 130 meters.

Chapter 9: The Origin Of The Mayan Calendar

The lifestyles in one shape or each different of a time recording device is characteristic of all evolved cultures - it's far essential to document critical events in the lifestyles of the rulers of the state, music the cycle of agricultural paintings and ceremonies of the twelve months, and mark the motion of heavenly our bodies. The fifty -year calendar cycle existed among all of the peoples of Mesoamerica, consisting of the Maya. This time reference system, probable courting back to ancient instances, includes two regular with mutational cycles. The duration of the kind of cycles changed into 260 days, and this machine became a complicated interconnection of 13-day periods superimposed on a cyclic series of twenty days, each of which has its call. Sometimes the term "Tzolkin" is likewise used to seek advice from this counting system.

For the Maya, the countdown of the 260-day cycle started out with the day Imish, which had the number one, accompanied by manner of the usage of the second one amount, the day Ik', the

1/3 Ak'bal, the fourth-day K'an, and so on, until the calendar reached the day Ben, which got here at variety 13. The next day in the calendar have become the day of Ish, which started a current thirteen-day cycle and, for that reason, acquired serial no 1, the day following it Men acquired serial range 2, and so forth.

With this scheme, the closing day of the 260-day cycle become the day of Ahau with serial range 13, and the whole cycle repeated, beginning with the day of Imish, all over again with number one. How this timing scheme arose stays a thriller, but the way it changed into used is plain. Each of the instances of the cycle modified into related to a few particular mind, and the entire route of the twenty-day cycles showed with mechanical readability what exactly want to reveal up inside the future and strictly regulated the existence of every the Maya themselves and all different peoples of Mesoamerica. Such a time reference tool still exists unchanged among some remoted peoples in southern Mexico and the Mayan mountain area.

Special priests carry out calculations that make sure an appropriate operation of this machine. Related to the 260-day calendar cycle is the 365-day "fuzzy yr," so named due to the truth the actual duration of the sun 12 months is prepared 1 / 4 of a daylonger. This situation makes us claim each fourth 12 months a leap year and upload one extra day to it just so there can be no mismatch a number of the calendar and the sun twelve months. The Mayan calendar in fact neglected this circumstance. Within this yr, there were 18 months of 20 days every, to which, at the prevent of the 12 months, a fearsome duration of five unlucky days modified into introduced. The Mayan New Year started out on the first of the month of Pop, observed via the second and zero.33 of that month, and so on.

However, the last day of the month did not undergo the ordinal quantity 20 but a unique sign indicating the "transition of manipulate" to the following month in order, that is associated with Mayan philosophy, which believed that the affect of any man or woman time c language is felt before this period takes area. , and keeps for a certain quantity of time after its very last touch.

From all that has been said, it follows that every day had a date similar to it, each steady with the 260-day calendar cycle and the "fuzzy three hundred and sixty five days" calendar device. For example, the number one day of K'an in a 260-day cycle can also be Pop's first day of the month. Such a twist of destiny of dates, while the first K'an modified into the number one of the month Pop, befell as soon as in 18,980 days, in a period equal to fifty two "fuzzy years". This length is referred to as the "calendar circle". It is the handiest tool of counting years that the peoples of mountain Mexico have a tool with apparent shortcomings whilst connection with intervals exceeding fifty- years is needed to document sports. Although the Long Count calendar is usually called the Mayan calendar, in the classical length and even in in advance times, this calendar modified into very giant within the lowlands of Mesoamerica. But the Maya, who lived in the important vicinity, delivered this gadget to the very first-class diploma of accuracy.

This calendar is a totally one of a kind counting system, additionally primarily based on regular with mutational cycles, however the ones cycles are good-bye that, in evaluation to the "calendar circle," any of the events that befell during historic time may be recorded with none worry. That there is probably ambiguity within the information of dates. Instead of the usage of the "fuzzy yr" as the concept for the "prolonged depend" calendar, the Maya and extraordinary peoples used the Tun, a period of 360 days. The cycle of the calendar year looked like this: 20 Kin - 1 Uinal, or 20 days; 18 Winals - 1 Tun, or 360 days; 20 Tuns - 1 K'atun, or 7200 days; 20 K'atun - 1 Baktun, or 140 4,000 days.

The "Long Count" calendar dates recorded thru the Maya on their monuments embody the cycles cited, from longest to shortest, in descending order of significance. Each of those cycles has its numerical coefficient. All the ones durations need to be delivered as plenty as accumulate the vast kind of days that have surpassed because the end of the very last huge cycle. A length identical in duration to 13 Baktuns, the give up date of which fell on the day that is in the calendar circle corresponded to the first day of Ahau and the eighth day of the month Kumhu while counting steady with the 365-day cycle of the "fuzzy 3 hundred and sixty 5 days". Thus, the date traditionally recorded via the Maya as nine.10.19.Five.11, the tenth day of Chuen at the 4th of the month of Kumhu, may be calculated as follows: 9 Baktuns - 1,296,000 days 10 K'atuns - seventy ,000 days 19 Tuns - 6840 days five Uinals - one hundred days eleven Kins - eleven days Total 1,374,951 days. Exactly such quite a few days have passed from the give up of the final calendar cycle until the day got here, regular with the calendar circle corresponds to the date: the primary day of Chuen on the 4th day of the month Kumhu.

Here it's far essential to provide an explanation for the numerical coefficients of the calendar themselves. The Mayans and some extraordinary peoples of the plains, especially the Mixtec human beings of the Oaxaca Valley, have an extremely clean numeral system the use of most effective 3 symbols: a dot for one, a horizontal bar for five, and a stylized shell for zero. Numerals as a whole lot as four inclusive are indicated thru using dots. To suggest the variety 6, a dash modified into drawn, above which one dot became positioned, and 10 changed into indicated the usage of horizontal stripes.

The largest coefficient used in the calendar, the variety 19, changed into depicted using 4 dots above three horizontal traces The designation of numbers over 19, for the recording of which it turned into tremendously important to have the idea of "0."

Chapter 10: Gods

In mythology, gods are strong and often mystical beings vital to terrific cultures' ideals, memories, and customs. Most of the time, those divine beings are established to have specific powers, like shaping the sector, affecting natural activities, and finding out human beings's fates. In one-of-a-type international locations and instances, gods represent severa things, like awareness, energy, love, or perhaps mischief. They are the primary characters in myths, legends, and non secular tales.

People take a look at the tales and reminiscences approximately the gods to determine out their characteristic in explaining the unidentified, coaching ethical instructions, and keeping society in order. These stories offer humans want, direction, and on occasion fear. In mythology, gods inform recollections that specify human nature, the enigmas of lifestyles, and the complex connections amongst humans and the gods. This economic destroy discusses those divine gods' notable additives and functions, that specialize in how they may be related to herbal sports, human emotions, and social norms. This financial disaster offers an extensive and interesting take a look at the divine through breaking down the complicated testimonies of gods in mythology. It offers readers a deep data of the thoughts and beliefs which have modified this mythology.

Mesoamerican cultures that got here in advance than and determined them. During the Classical Period of Mayan civilization, which lasted from 250 AD to 900 AD, spiritual mind reached their whole development. The Mayan pantheon had over one hundred gods and no longer many ladies. Some of the Mayan gods were accompanied thru later civilizations, similar to the Aztecs, who used some of them of their private pantheon.

During the Late Pre-Classic time, before 250 AD, the Mayan religion took its first steps. It grew into a totally-fledged religion at some point of the Classic Period, which lasted from 250 AD to 900 AD. Throughout this time, hieroglyphic writing commenced, and there had been many holy writings at the pyramids and temples inside the area. Also, there are various signs and symptoms and signs and signs of sacrifice for the duration of the Classic Period, along with sacrifices of human beings. The faith lived on after the Mayans fell apart in the post-Classic duration and impacted distinct Mesoamerican civilizations.

Among the Mayan gods and goddesses, there had been many. However, some had been the maximum powerful. One of the maximum vital Mayan gods modified into Chac, who end up in price of rain, thunder, childbirth, and farming. Kinich Ahau and Ahaw Kin changed into the call of the Mayan solar god. He come to be additionally one of the sturdy Mayan gods. Yumil Kaxob have emerge as the decision of the Mayan corn god. He changed into moreover crucial because of the reality maize become the Mayans' primary meals supply. For a number of the ones gods, unique sacrifices have been made, collectively with killing human beings as an providing.

In the Mayan faith, monks executed a big role due to the truth they were seen as flow-betweens for the human beings and the gods and goddesses. A lot of the time, clergymen dressing up as gods led non secular ceremonies and celebrations. Mayan clergymen moreover took element inside the workout of sacrificing people. They were greater or a whole lot tons less on the identical degree as the the Aristocracy due to the truth clergymen had been essential to the Mayan faith.

Just like within the religions related to amazing Mesoamerican cultures, spiritual symbols were awesome to the Mayans. The Mayan goddesses and deities had been regularly validated in strategies that showed how effective they had been. To represent the god of rain, Chac, as an example, artists have drawn him with the talents of a frog and tears coming from his eyes. In the identical way, the god of mortality was established with one among a kind bone decorations. Several Mayan codices supply an reason for the non secular meanings of the gods and goddesses of the Maya.

Mayans concept that once they died, people moved to the Underworld, ruled through many gods, some more potent than others. This must best appear to those who died giving begin or had been killed. But it is possible that the Mayans by no means had a unmarried concept of what takes region after loss of life. Another concept the Mayans had changed into that much less high priced humans may work to paradise after they died. Dangerous people, on the alternative, have been despatched to the underground to be tortured all the time. This modified into the decision of the god of loss of existence and the Underworld. Even even though he became the tremendous and maximum effective god inside the Underworld, the Underworld emerge as moreover run with the aid of the use of different gods and their helpers.

Rituals for Mayan goddesses and deities have been closely connected to the kings of the united states. During the Maya Classic Period, kingship practices have been critical because of the fact people belief kings were descended from gods. People concept kings' blood changed into holy, so letting blood flow end up a regular royal ritual. Because human blood changed into visible as holy, the sacrifice of kings come to be additionally extra treasured, and seized members from the enemy royal family have been used as sacrifices. Religious ceremonies had been additionally held while a king died or have emerge as a king.

The Mayan goddesses and deities had many tales about how they dealt with each different, much like people. Mayan folklore has many critical memories approximately how the earth grow to be made, how notable plants have been given their names, how time works, and the manner the arena will quit. The sun, the Mayan paintings, and substantial artefacts hold a outstanding deal statistics approximately their myths.

Calendar mapping, sacrifices and services, praying, and pilgrimages had been important to the Mayan religion. People used spells and songs with saints, angels, and gods during prayers. As part of beliefs and traditions, human beings did various things to get smooth. This intended no longer ingesting, bathing, or having sexual own family contributors. People went on pilgrimages to one-of-a-type locations which have been crucial to them religiously.

Regarding Mayan deities and goddesses, the concept of sacrifice have turn out to be essential. Mayan mythology says the gods gave up elements of their our our bodies or even their lives to make the area. As a manner to reveal thanks, people made sacrifices. This blanketed giving meals and topics as provides, lowering someone open, and, most significantly, killing someone as a sacrifice. Although human sacrifice wasn't as important to them as to the Aztecs, it turned into although carried out in a unique way.

In pyramid temples, the Mayans worshipped and did many non secular practices and ceremonies. It became possible to worship Mayan goddesses and deities in distinct types of houses. The first, a unmarried, had a flat top in which the temple changed into built. This constructing modified into used for non secular activities, and those had been regularly killed as sacrifices there. The different type of pyramid did not have a flat top and have become additionally now not very huge. People idea this tower changed into holy and shouldn't be touched.

This is because of the truth the Mayans believed in plenty of gods and goddesses, and people everywhere in the nation worshipped them. There were splendid gods like Kinich Ahau, who modified into in charge of dying and the Underworld, and Chac, who have become in charge of rain and fertility. People finished many practices for the gods, which includes the maximum crucial one, which changed into killing someone as a sacrifice. Ceremonies and rituals have been led via the usage of monks, who had been very crucial in the Mayan religion.

Chapter 11: God Of Featherd Serpent

Kukulkan, additionally referred to as the winged or plumed snake god, have become part of the mythology and religious ideals of the Yucatec Maya humans in Mesoamerica. People concept that Kukulkan end up a maker who sent rain and winds, and is the reason why he showed up in lots of fantastic forms. He is attached to the temple at Chichen Itza, built in his honour. Kukulkan is likewise a large determine in Mexican way of life.

People in Mesoamerica believed that the snake have become a god who represented life on and underneath the ground and come to be associated with the Underworld. People additionally perception snakes lived in holes that brought on the Underworld because of how they lived. Several works of art work from the region additionally display the useless our bodies of the snakes above.

The terms "sky" and "snake" sound the identical in every English and Maya.

When humans in Yucatan speak about Kukulkan, they often suggest a one-of-a-type individual with the same name. This person, also known as Kukulkan, can also had been a king or priest of Chichen Itza inside the tenth century. In the 16th century, Kukulkan come to be seen as a historical determine. But in the 9th century, artefacts from Chichen Itza did now not display that he changed right into a herbal man or woman. Instead, they drew him proper proper into a vision of a snake wrapped throughout the our our our bodies of lords.

The name Kukulkan does a amazing manner of describing how he seems. What form of snake does he look like? A winged serpent. It is said that he has wings which could help him fly and communicate with the sun. In Mayan folklore, Kukulkan is a well-known god normally tested as a bird-like being that resembles someone. Different versions of this image show it as an ordinary snake or a snake with wings.

People gave starting to Kukulkan, a snake. He were given so large that his sister can also additionally no longer nurse him, so he loved leaving the underground place in which they raised him. The earth shakes due to this, and the snake does this each July to reveal his sister that he is though alive. The Aztecs, in addition to the human beings of Toltec, moreover known as him Quetzalcoatl, which means "snake god." The god modified into moreover called Ehecatl via the Gulf Coast companies and Gucumatz via way of the Maya in Guatemala.

Many pyramids had been embellished at some stage in the Mayan's significant woods to appear to be snakes. People constructed the ones places to make Kukulkan, who modified into seen as a vengeful god, satisfied. These systems were made to capture the moderate, and blood emerge as used to coloration in some unspecified time in the future of human sacrifice rituals.

Kukulkan made the area's four elements, but he despite the fact that guidelines over the wind. A essential stone that he owns is stated to symbolize the start of all air. He additionally delivered a calendar, a stone disk with numbers from prolonged within the beyond, and confirmed it to sincerely absolutely everyone. Sadly, the blood turned into used inside the services achieved for his gain.

Kukulkan stays the centre of have a have a look at and discovery at many Mayan web sites, together with Chichen Itza, together with more pyramids from the vintage Mayan empire that have been surely lately positioned. Kukulkan has moreover been in a season of the cool lively movie show Star Trek and is someone in video video video games together with Smite and Tomb Raider.

Itzamna: Mayan Creator of th Universe

In Mayan mythology, Itzamna is seen collectively with the maximum terrific gods. He is notion to have created the world and is the daddy of the whole thing. Through certainly one of a kind memories, Itzamna is seen as a cultural hero who helped the Maya build their society. He taught those people a manner to make diaries, broaden corn, and be medical medical doctors. He additionally got here up with a way to divide the land.

There are many pix of Itzamna in Mayan writings, and he is likewise used to beautify many Mayan homes. Itzamna may be visible on one of the shrine structures on the Palenque ancient web site. Itzamna is a massive part of Mexican similarly to Mayan society. However, no longer many human beings beyond Mayan mythology realize approximately her.

Itzamna is the maximum crucial god inside the Mayan religion, and you can see him in locations like Palenque, Copan, and Stela 25. Before the Spanish came, he changed into confirmed in many books and clay models. At first, humans called him "god D." However, earlier than the Maya names had been determined out, some researchers known as him "god X."Many varieties of paintings, like wall art work, statues, and codexes, show Itzamna as an antique man sitting on a throne and going through top notch gods, like God L or N. In a few snap shots, he's moreover confirmed as a sage priest carrying a tall, flower-fashioned hat.

Itzamna is every so often called a - headed underwater snake or a creature that looks like a cross amongst a caiman and a person. Some human beings count on it shows what the Maya idea of due to the fact the reptilian shape of the world. The Bird of Heaven, also referred to as Itzam Yeh, is one of the most essential varieties of Itzamna. This chicken is often associated with Vucub Caquix, a monster from mythology killed through the use of the courageous ones Xbalanque and Hunapuh.

Maya legend says that Itzamná was a issue of the most powerful couple. He modified into married to the older version of the deity Ix Chel, additionally referred to as Goddess O, and the two of them had all of the one among a kind gods. Besides that, he have grow to be a little one of Hunab Ku, the Mayan god who made the arena. Itzamna have become the ancestor of Bacab, a four-headed god dwelling deep within the earth. In a unique story, Itzamna and Ix Chel had 13 youngsters, of whom made the area and those.

Itzamna is a Mayan word meaning a large seafood, a caiman, or a few component corresponding to a snake. According to Nahuatl and Quechua, the "Itz" a part of his call can suggest masses of various topics, like "cloud stuff," "divination," or "anticipate earlier." There are many names for Itzamna, like

Kukulcan and Itzam Caban, however scientists name him God D.

You can consider Itzamna as a author in the testimonies because he makes tactics and structures that are only clinical or rational. A story says that Itzamna confirmed the Maya the way to make calendars. The Maya used unique kinds of calendars sooner or later of this time. They had a 260-day calendar and a calendar with 365 that became just like the Gregorian calendar. They additionally made a calendar that went from 1960 to 2020. The Maya applied those information to discern out the incredible days to do numerous things, like farming and attending church. They moreover made some distinct cultural statistics.

People say that Itzamna brought new mind in technological expertise and generation to the Maya. People see him as a crucial stress that brings collectively the factors of hell, earth, and heaven. In the situation of Yucatan after the classical duration, Itzamna come to be seen as a restoration deity. People have been regularly unwell during this time with such things as hypersensitive reactions and chills.

Most researchers, further to Ancient Astronaut theorists, start their paintings at Itzamna. They suppose that the Mayan society changed into one of the first to do many great scientific studies of lifestyle that have changed the world. People global are constantly interested by and afraid of the Mayan calendar because of the faux notion that the area will surrender whilst their timetable does. People say that Itzamna made this calendar, and he or she or he finally ends up being the primary challenge depend of communicate. A man or woman from

Marvel Comics end up moreover based on Itzamna and his abilities.

Yum Kaax: God of Forest and Wildlife

Oh, Kaax is the decision of the god of woods and animals, and he often watches over such things as farming and looking. People have unique thoughts approximately whether or no longer he and Ah Mun are the identical god or separate gods. Assuming they will be gods, Yum Kaax may want to appearance out for the earth, and Ah Mun could be chargeable for farming and maize. In the Mayan documents, which might be agencies of folding books, Ah Mun is the name of the god of woods and animals. He is the equal god as E.

Some matters make Yum Kaax outstanding from extraordinary Mayan gods, regardless of the reality that he resembles them. For instance, he is often proven in carvings, drawings, and engravings as a more youthful, lovable man or woman who marks the start of the developmental cycle of flora and animals. People generally anticipate that this photograph suggests Ah Mun and Yum Kaax because it shows them holding corn ears. You might also need to appearance it as a photograph of Ah Mun and Yum Kaax. People assume that the primary one is a type god who could no longer have a horrible popularity.

When hooked up bodily, he is often a extra youthful man carrying a hat with blue and yellow bands and the shape of a corn cob. Many people see him protective a bowl with all three ears of corn. He is likewise referred to as the ruler of forests. Mayan writings say his extended locks and appropriate appears make him a stunning god. Mayan texts from the Yucatan, Mexico area say that

God Yum Kaax end up the kid of the extremely good gods Itzamn and Ixchel. He have come to be moreover one of the youngest gods, and the Jungle have become his mission to study over them. The Maya phrases "Yum," because of this "lord," and "Kaax," due to this "the wild," are wherein the god of woods and flora and fauna receives his name. It manner "lord of forests." People assume this name for the god has been acquainted for a long time.

Before Columbus came to America, the Maya believed the god of woods modified into essential. Farmers frequently call on his call to maintain wild animals out in their fields and deliver him their first flowers, normally logs lessen from the wooded place. In the woods, hunters regularly removed their shirt sleeves and laid them out over numerous floor stakes to look for deer.

People suppose that this is a ritual that includes Yum Kaax.

God Yum Kaax regarded out for hunters in addition to animals. They might also need to commonly ask the gods to defend them and permit them to are seeking earlier than they went. They could get in hassle with him if they will be suggest or careless. People knew that the god of climate appeared out for Yum Kaax. The Mayans believed that rain changed into an critical a part of human and vegetation, so that they determined it as a god.

People though worship the god of climate and wooden these days, regardless of the truth that the faith-primarily based definitely cult that used to exist not exists. People do no longer worship the Maya gods as lots as they used to, but hunters although do the rite in advance than they pass looking. A story says a hunter should get lost inside the bush if he does not ask Juan T'ul for permission first. It is probably stable for them to head returned home, but the wild may furthermore however motive them to lose a few subjects. Juan T'ul idea that God Yum Kaax regarded out for the lives of animals inside the wild. Names and memories about the spirit alternate from region to place, but most people do not forget him a determine god.

Chaac: God of Rain

In historical times, the Yucatán vicinity of Mexico, recognized due to its rain, had a god known as Chaac who have become proven with massive spherical eyes, a nostril that appeared like a proboscis, and tooth that stuck out. Like one of a kind vital Mayan gods, he have end up modified right into a circle of relatives of gods known as the Chacs. The four factors of the compass—red, white, yellow, and black—had been related to those gods. In the time after the Classic, some human beings had a reputation for providing their bodies to make peace with the rain god. Priests inside the Chichén Itza area had been known as chaacs due to the reality they held the patients' arms and legs. The Chaacs Mool changed proper right into a god worshipped internal Toltec and Mayan net websites.

According to Mayan legend, the god Chaac had a unique look. His frame became generally a human with scales from a frog or reptile, and his head have emerge as normally not human, with an extended nose and fangs that caught out. In the traditional fashion, he wore a shell round his ear. The god modified into furthermore said for having a protracted tongue and a nose that changed into hooked. His nose become pointing up, making it seem like an elephant's nostril. He have become also shown with animal capabilities, like scales, that might advise he emerge as related to fish or reptiles. He changed into regularly confirmed with jade swords and snakes in his fingers, which he threw on the clouds to make it rain.

In the Mayan tale approximately the Sun and Moon, the god of rain, Chaac, is the younger brother of the god Sun. They beat their vintage adopted mother and the person she is seeing. In the surrender, Chaac, the rain god, is punished for having a courting together alongside along with his brother's partner. His tears of ache made it rain. Various renditions of this story say that the rain god used his lightning bolt to chase after the Moon and Sun as they ran away.

The rain god Chaac is one among many Mayan gods related to trees. A tale says that he changed into one of the people who helped damage down a rock to find out maize. This rain have become important to the Mayas as it gave them water for developing plants and ingesting.

It became not unusual for people in the Yucatec area to preserve a night meal to honour the god Chaac. At this prevalence, four boys should located on a show to make the god satisfied. In the 1600s, humans moreover did comparable practices. The young women and men had been regularly thrown into the underground cenotes. The sufferers have been on occasion left to sink to the lowest of a cenote and die, and specific instances, they were discovered revived lower once more to lifestyles. People idea parents who've been pulled out of the cenote had won powers. Chaac is a individual in Smite that may be utilized as a fighter. In the sport Final Fantasy 10, a Kucumatz enemy man or woman and the Chaac creature have decrease-degree versions that you can play as.

In mythology, goddesses are reputable, frequently airy beings who play critical factors in the recollections and non secular beliefs of humans global. These holy girl beings have precise traits beginning from disturbing and motherly to fierce and mysterious. Goddesses have stood for things like creation, fertility, information, and protection in many nations and instances.

They are respected as examples of the electricity and goodness of women, who form fates, change the cycles of nature, and lead the manner for humans. In myths, legends, and spiritual testimonies, gods display us the numerous sides of being a woman, the mysteries of the universe, and the deep ties between human beings and the divine. Myths about them frequently mirror societal ideals and thoughts of what it method to be a lady, which gives us a glimpse into how males and females interacted in the beyond. This economic catastrophe explores mythology's fascinating global of goddesses, searching at their roles, trends, and meanings in specific vintage cultures.

Ix Chel: Moon Goddess

Ixchel, also written as Ix Chel, became the call of a lady jaguar goddess within the ancient Maya society who changed into in price of medication and childbirth.

She is set up to Toci Yoalticitl, an Aztec goddess residing in a sweat tub. The Mayan lunar goddess O is associated with the god Ixchel, moreover written as Ix Chel. Ixchel modified into pictured as an unpleasant vintage lady with evil traits and the goddess of crafts for girls. Ixchel modified into visible as a codical god in a contemporary update to the Schellhas-Zimmermann kind.

People count on Ix Chel turn out to be part of the mythical god Itzamna. The Maya those who lived on the peninsula of Mexico saw her as a goddess associated with the moon, water, giving shipping, and weaving. She is furthermore the girl shape of all Mayan gods and possesses suggestions about how existence and loss of existence work. As the father or mom of souls, Ixchel is constantly converting from a pretty more youthful lady to an antique witch who stocks the data of her humans.

Ix Chel also can need to change into distinct bureaucracy. There's a danger that some of her factors were photos of different queens. There are moreover main topics approximately her that most human beings agree on. Ix Chel turn out to be frequently showed as an older woman carrying traditional Mayan garments and a snake crown. In this tale, she should likely have worn an beneath overlaying the dress's bones. It grow to be said that she had talons on her fingers and ft. A frightening mouth and a huge earthen jar have been not unusual methods to show Ix Chel. Ix Chel grow to be now and again tested to be a younger female. She seemed lovable and wore a hat. On pinnacle of her mouth, the forestall of her beak have emerge as additionally seen. Ix Chel's younger self regularly seems in a friendlier moderate than her older self.

The most crucial factor in her circle of relatives's data grow to be whilst she had been given married. In some Mayan recollections, she had been given hitched to Votan; in others, she had been married to its call. She has thirteen boys within the memories of Shex Chel and Itzamna. One of these deities is Bacab, a Mayan god who bears the sky in his fingers. The four Bacabs could have been the handiest children of Shex Chel in addition to Itzamna as nicely. Ix Chel have turn out to be linked to Hun Hunahpu, the corn god. It's not clear whether or not or no longer he was one of her 13 boys, however he end up stated to have preferred assist to be reborn.

People in particular locations have called Ix Chel great names, consisting of The Queen, Goddess Rainbow, Hawk Woman, Our Mama, the White Ladies, Goddess of Becoming, Earth Mother, the Womb, the Cave for Life, Guardian of the Bones, and extra. People believed that as a fertility deity, she may also want to make big storms appear. It is unknown if she may also moreover need to bring about failures or if she became the reason the seasons changed. She is thought to have controlled her waters thru a jar that turn out to be grew to emerge as the opposite manner up, no matter how they were used. Because she come to be a weaver, Ix Chel made the right wheel on the middle of the entirety. It's not clean what she did on this a part of the area, but she modified into amazing.

Chapter 12: Mythical Creatures

In mythology, legendary animals are imaginary and regularly out-of-this-worldwide beings that live within the worlds of imagination and folklore. These charming animals are a combination of human, animal, and supernatural factors that push the boundaries of the natural global. They are essential elements of the myths and legends of many remarkable cultures. They have trends and logos that display how complex human feelings, fears, and hopes are. Mythical animals like dragons, tricksters, and proper spirits capture our imaginations and assist us percent cultural information, inform memories, and precise ourselves via artwork. In unique cultures, those creatures display how the human mind can recollect some element and the way ideals make up a complicated net that has changed societies at some point of information.

But the ones animals had been referred to extensively in traditions, legends, fables, writing, mythology, fairy-story novels, myths, and other kinds of fiction. People who agree with in realism say that stories approximately magical creatures have existed prolonged in advance than information have come to be a technological understanding. People have an entire lot of outstanding views and mind approximately mythical beasts, which results in many extremely good theories approximately whether or not or not they exist. This detail shows a huge agency of thrilling legendary creatures that make you need to realise more.

Nagual: Supernatural Jaguar

A nagual, moreover referred to as nahual, is an Indian discern spirit from Mesoamerica. In some locations, sturdy guys can alternate into the nagual animal to do lousy things. The word comes from the Nahuatl phrase nahualli, which refers to the creatures that sorcerers can tackle magically. When someone gets their nagual, they typically bypass someplace by myself till they wake up. People in a few cultures come to be linked to their nagual even as they may be a toddler, and the nagual is the primary animal that crosses over the kid's ashes. Different additives of the area have one in every of a type beliefs about nagualism. Some locations count on that naguals are excellent owned via manner of the maximum influential leaders. In some, all or most humans have animal determine powers.

Naguals have each strong and weak factors. The characteristics of these creatures are linked to the day someone modified into born. Say a person modified into born on Dog Day. That character must have each sturdy and vulnerable aspects, like a canine. In Mexico, individuals who get a nagual are concept to want to make a cope with the satan for it to be seen as a gift. This animal can change into a wolf, a dog, or a hen at night time time. If the nagual is in human shape, they appear to be some different person, commonly a person. Some records say that they trade right into a jaguar, at the same time as others say that they handiest start to expose a few dispositions of the holy animal.

Navajo terms nagual and nahualli every imply "transforming witch." The English word for this is regularly "shapeshifter." It is likewise written as nahual in loads of

English texts. People expect Naguals are as robust as werewolves because they may combat similarly. They are also concept to were made thru the use of the god Tezcatlipoca.

In assessment to werewolves, anybody can with out problems alternate into a nagual on every occasion they want to. But, just like people, those creatures need unique competencies and highbrow durability to put off their curse. Naguals normally alternate once they feel threatened, underneath a whole lot stress, or if they may be round evil, but it varies on what kind of person was cursed to emerge as a nagual.

Tsukán: Giant Snake

In August 2006, it changed into an overcast day. Gabriela Rivas Ochoa were on her way home from supporting her aunt run a small grocery store and restaurant on the edge of the metropolis of Calcehtok, which is about twenty-five miles south-east of Mérida, the capital of the Mexican kingdom of Yucatán. Young Gabriela heard moving within the thick vegetation through the street. Her associate and youngsters and near buddies have been scared thru what she said she located, however the older people in the city had been not. Gabriela stated she noticed a darkish-colored snake with fluff or fur on top of its skull. Its body modified into thick as an alrighttrunk. She remarkable observed the issue in brief as it speedy slithered away. Some people in town idea Gabriela made the story to get hobby or have a have a look at topics. Some human beings idea it became a change or a natural event that randomly triggered the snake to get so big. While most of the human beings in this metropolis were natives, the leaders knew higher and have been now not scared. Some laughed and suggested the human beings round them not to worry. Many older human beings were happy to appearance the massive protect snake due to the truth they hadn't heard tales approximately it in a long term.

From the Yucatec Maya language, "Tsukán" comes from "tsuk," which means "horse," and "kaan," which means that that that "snake." Some versions of the tale say this snake's head is as massive as a horse's. However, language experts say the word "horse" in this Maya community comes from the identical root due to the fact the phrase for the silky ends of ripe corn covering the stalk. The Mayans believed that horses' manes and ponytails appeared much like the clean fibres located at the ends of cornhusks after they first got here to the Yucatán. The Tsukán's head can be as large as a horse's, but the "tsuk" comes from a pre-Hispanic phrase for corn silk, which seems to be coming out of its head and lower lower back.

There is not any document of the manner lengthy the tale of Tsukán is going again, however it is idea to be loads of years vintage. It's crucial to understand that this substantial snake is part of the mythology of the northern Yucatán, and those say they've got visible it nowadays. If you trust the tale, there can be a couple of Tsukán for each cave or cenote. This is due to the truth they may be the guardians of these places. As for the Maya, the Tsukán is neither a god nor a spirit. Instead, they see it as extra of a effective being with unique abilties, just like the skinny Jungle. The Maya named the Sisimite a bigfoot-like creature that watched over and guarded the cenotes and caves. The Tsukán's interest is to make sure that the cenotes and caves generally have enough water. People are not dangerous to the Tsukán and do no longer mind that human beings are in their area. In the northwest of Yucatán, there may be a tale about a farmer who decided on to rest via using manner of sitting on what he believed to be a huge log, which became out to be a downed tree.

When the log commenced out to move, the farmer jumped up in fear. He have emerge as spherical and determined the Tsukán gently slither away, now not being worried that a person modified into the usage of it as a makeshift bed. The Tsukán will generally live a long way from humans, however it will combat if it feels threatened clearly and robustly. It is said that everybody who kills one could have lousy fulfillment. If you observe a

Tsukán inside the wild, the extremely good detail to do is to leave it by myself. The person experiencing this have to apprehend that this massive creature's best reason is to assist, so there is not a few component to worry. Little animals are what the Tsukán eats, and they determine on magpies, which the Maya referred to as "cheel." When the Tsukán wishes something to devour, it spreads its mouth extensive. The warmth from the breath kills and breaks down some of its meals. It makes me do not forget a dragon that breathes hearth on a smaller scale. When the Tsukán receives antique, it gets feathers and wings and soars to the sea to die. Following this, a logo-new, younger Tsukán will take over due to the fact the parent of that cave or cenote.

The interesting story of procedures the Tsukán came to be has been surpassed down from technology to technology.

The story begins while the Maya u . S . A . Has a bad drought, and the Maya weather god Chaac is concerned. Chaac's method have become to get water from underground belongings and bring it to the Maya towns. To get water from above, the desperate climate god flew on the back of a reptile with wings corresponding to a Pteranodon and Pterodactyl. Chaac's desired rivers, lakes, and cenotes have been dry, which made him sad. He and his flying lizard decided on to relaxation on a huge log in a forest that had dried out. But, just like in the story about the farmer, the log started to move, and Chaac and his flying reptile pal short determined out they had been sitting in a massive snake.

Because Chaac understood that Tsukán may also want to heal himself all of the time, he tricked the big snake. As Tsukán walked once more within the path of the cenotes, he hit Chaac together collectively together with his body and knocked him to the ground. But the deity of rain waved the whip. It made a thunderclap, right away killing the snake and turning him into hundreds of water drops that fell onto the cenotes. Once extra, water crammed the streams, caves, and cenotes. Down in a cave, the water drops slowly came collectively until they formed the shape of a snake, which grew and were given wings yet again. Instead of going to the ocean, Tsukán left his steady area and ran into Chaac. Chaac hit him with a strong gust of wind. Tsukán come to be the rain again because of the unexpected blast of air. The snake with the mane and wings continuously desired to transport once more to the sea. However, he modified into cursed to die and reincarnate over and over virtually so the cenotes, caves, and wells of Yucatán might normally have sufficient water.

People dwelling inside the north Yucatán Peninsula have typically gotten their water from cenotes, caves, and wells because the island is fabricated from rock and has no on foot water. Researchers who take a look at folklore and different subjects say that the story regarding Tsukán is meant to help people loosen up approximately the shortage of water. An severe and magical being is in charge of the story and is a mother or father and defender. When some thing as important as water is in the care of an animal this clever, you don't have any purpose to stress due to the fact everything is probably ok. By protecting the water supply, the Tsukán moreover protects all residing matters, at the facet of the animals and plants that the Maya rely on for meals.

La Xtabay: Demonic Feme Fatel

The Yucatec Maya have a story referred to as La Xtabay approximately a monster woman who kills men inside the Yucatán Peninsula. She is thought to live inside the bush and use her beautiful beauty to trap guys into their deaths. It is stated that she wears a white dress and has lovely, vivid black hair which falls to her feet.

Xkeban and Utz-colel have been adorable girls who lived in a village or town on the Yucatán Peninsula. People from time to time say that the women are sisters. People in Xkeban's society didn't like her because of the truth she modified into promiscuous. However, they notion Utz-colel modified into precise because of the truth he stayed single. The villagers have been going to ship Xkeban away, however they decided directly to preserve her to make her experience even worse about herself. Even despite the fact that she became mistreated, Xkeban helped the terrible, the sick, and animals which have been in need. Utz-colel, as a substitute, end up cold-hearted and concept she come to be higher than anyone round her, especially folks who had been socially decrease than her. People inside the city loved Utz-colel due to the fact she changed into unmarried and failed to care that she became mean.

A few days after Xkeban died, the people of the metropolis located her body surrounded through flora that smelled accurate. The homeless and awful human beings that Xkeban helped all through her life held funerals for her. Soon after, a remarkable, sweet-smelling blossom grew round her grave due to the truth Xkeban had changed proper right into a shape of morning glory called xtabentún in the Maya language. Xtabentún is a lazy, clinging vine that spreads via hedges, filling the air with the fragrance of its touchy white trumpets. It is said to are seeking out for safe haven in hedges due to the reality it is defenceless, similar to Xkeban felt even as she have become human. A drink with the identical name due to the truth the flower is crafted from it. Ipomoea corymbosa additionally have come to be one of the most well-known entheogens a number of the Aztecs. They known as the plant coaxihuitl in Nahuatl and the psychoactive seeds ololiúqui. The Zapotecs even though use the seeds to create recuperation trances of their recovery rituals in recent times.

Utz-Colel have grow to be proud to suppose that because of the fact she have become so herbal, her useless body became going to heady scent better than Xkeban's. However, her vain frame smelled lousy. The complete metropolis got here to her funeral and left vegetation round her tomb which have been long past tomorrow. Utz-colel changed into the flower on the Tzacam plant that smells horrible. Utz-colel offered prayers to evil spirits, who granted her want to grow to be a female over again to become a cute blossom in loss of existence. But because of the fact she couldn't love and end up most effective pushed via manner of way of anger and jealousy, she modified into the demon Xtabay, who appeared like a cute girl yet modified into mean and predatory.

Camazotz: Giant Vampire

This horrifying creature from Mayan mythology changed into stated to be a enormous vampire bat that have turn out to be as big as a complete-grown human male or perhaps extra vast. It may strike within the midnight and suck the blood out of its sufferers. Like a real bat, he great ventured out at night time time to scare the people inside the place. During the day, the populace of Maya idea this monster modified into secure because of the reality he have grow to be perception to be hiding someplace as a rock statue. People residing in Central America feared this full-size, bloodthirsty vampire bat. It had a popularity for killing and ingesting the blood of both human beings and animals. People even stated he killed all of the Mayan people as part of a slaughter. There are many gods and monsters in historical Mayan mythology. The gods stored the Mayans slaves and locked them up in Xibalba, the

Underworld, to protect them from great monsters.

The gods asked the Mayans to make sacrifices. In exchange for their protection, the Mayans regularly needed to kill and blood-sacrifice humans. Some ancient Mayans in the long run rose towards those regulations and the merciless gods' felony tips. The gods despatched Camazotz some distance from Xibalba and onto the earth as a punishment. It have become said that this mythical demon killed off the entire Mayan race so that the deities ought to make a state-of-the-art race of human beings that might study their hints and legal guidelines.

This huge vampire bat changed into evil as hell. People say that whilst he modified into in the Underworld, he led his troops in fierce fights with the Mayan gods and stopped them from stepping into the Underworld.

Chapter 13: Legends

A legend is an vintage tale or series of reminiscences about someone or region. The phrase "legend" meant a story about a holy individual. According to legends, memories about supernatural beings, mythical creatures, or natural sports are just like folktales in what they are saying. However, legends are precise to a place or man or woman and are recommended as ancient statistics.

Mythology research memories that combine information, creativeness, and traditional ideals. These testimonies are known as legends. In the ones reminiscences, ordinary human beings, places, or things regularly skip the road among fact and the supernatural. Legends are informed from technology to generation, becoming a large part of a community's identity and manner of sharing recollections. On the alternative hand, many close by memories are simply well-known testimonies connected to a specific individual or location.

Whether they may be approximately heroic acts, the origins of herbal landmarks, or the lives of well-known people, these reminiscences show what people charge, what they desire for, and what makes life mysterious. Mythology's legends are a hyperlink a number of the regular and the great. They remind humans in their past and display how human beings are the same in the course of time and global locations.

The Aluxes

Trolls, elves, and goblins populate this global. It appears that each civilization has given those enchanted beings their call. They are referred to as aluxes by way of manner of the Maya humans, and they may be described as little entities that stay in jungles and emerge from their houses at night to bring about hassle for disrespectful human beings. Tradition has it that to appease the Aluxes and stay out of their awful graces, one should collect a miniature house for them and present them with inconsequential services, together with food, wine, or maybe smoke. This will make sure that they'll be content and will offer an extraordinary fortune to humans.

In the Yucatán Peninsula, there are numerous testimonies approximately Aluxes. Some human beings in Lepán say they heard those people in a cenote. They say it have end up late at night time time, no person else have emerge as round, and the sounds have been unmistakable. People in Laguna Om, it really is in addition south, tell a story about a toddler stranded within the woods. After three days, he again in a unmarried piece, telling tales about children inside the bush that helped him move returned.

Things have lengthy beyond wrong in Cancún, too. People who stay within the region understand that the span that connects the accommodations repute quo Zone to the airport saved falling aside on the same time as it become being built. They should artwork at the suspension bridge at a few degree inside the day, but their paintings have become long long beyond when they were given home within the morning.

They decided to speak with a Maya a priest, who informed them that they had to appease the aluxes to accumulate permission to bring collectively. Now, each time you stress under that bridge, preserve a near be careful for something suspicious. A miniature pyramid may be observed tucked away inside the back of the flyover on the road's western side. That is the place of the fluxes and the most effective motive why the bridge has now not collapsed.

Mayan Tree of Life

Many vintage myths have the same crucial concept: the tree of lifestyles. This is likewise actual of Mayan lore. The Tree of Life, which the Mayans known as Yaxche, fashioned an vital a part of how they observed the universe. The Mayans noticed the branch of lifestyles as an picture of the form in their universe. They idea that it related the 3 vital components of their universe: the religious realm, the physical international, and Xibalba, the Mayan call for hell. In the vintage Mayan story of Hero Twins, there is a tree that gives existence as a topic. In the tale, the father who had the twins had been murdered with the useful resource of the lords of the Underworld, and his head modified into caught in a useless tree branch. The tree again to existence and gave them fruit like their father's head.

The lords inside the Underworld had been terrified of the tree's power and advised no character to transport near it. At a few element, a infant of one of the Xibalba lords went as much as the tree, and the fruit made her pregnant. After that, she rose from the depths of the arena and gave upward thrust to the hero twins there. The holy tree of existence is confirmed in artwork in the Mayan city of Palenque. These pictures show that the Mayans sacrificed animals and their juice to the holy tree of lifestyles. It moreover shows the kings who dominated the Mayan town within the past, honouring the tree that sustains life and giving it gives. A well-known instance of this type of artwork may be seen inside the grave of a Palenque king from the 7th century.

In Mayan legend, the 4 number one hints completed a good sized position. They have been additionally associated with the Mayan cowl of life at once. The

Mayans belief the holy tree of existence spread in all 4 instructions. Because of this, the Mayans had awesome thoughts approximately all four commands. They said the 4 winds had been staffed via 4 forms of the climate god, the four Chacs. In each a part of the area, those Chacs held up the vicinity of heaven above the ground. That's why humans concept the tree packed with life would likely expand leaves in all four pointers to spread lifestyles.

As established within the legend of the Hero Twins and specific Mayan myths, the Mayans idea that the holy tree of life came from the Underworld. They said the tree started lifestyles, which started on earth and unfold to the actual international. Mayans notion the sacred tree controlled time and area inside the real international. They additionally notion the tree had been given taller and taller until it reached heaven, in which it set the celestial our bodies in motion and helped shape the Mayan universe. In this manner, the Mayans idea that the holy tree of life linked and managed all three components of their worldwide.

The Mayans noticed the Ceiba trunk as a real-lifestyles illustration of the holy tree of lifestyles. Because of this, the Ceiba tree was usually planted at some stage in all Mayan towns and settlements. An not unusual Ceiba tree has a long, immediately trunk, and bats stay within the roots, it is incredible. The Mayans notion the straight away, prolonged trunk symbolised the horizontal line that related remarkable worlds. Last however no longer least, the Ceiba tree has a protective of leaves that spreads out in all 4 suggestions. This have become what the Mayans notion stood for the 4 recommendations. People in spite of the truth that increase the tree inside the center of Mayan cities, wherein it is concept to have been used for essential spiritual ceremonies.

There is so much space inner a ceiba tree's roots that they feel like big caves. Bats regularly live in these roots, such as to the idea that the Ceiba tree represents God's Tree of Life. This is because of the fact, in Mayan folklore, bats are frequently linked to the Underworld. In the story knowledgeable thru the Hero Twins, one of the bat gods killed each of them at the same time as they had been on a journey in the Underworld. In this manner, the reality that bats stay inside the roots of a Ceiba tree seems eerily much like the Mayan trunk of lifestyles from mythology.

Some specialists say that when the Spanish got here, the Christian go have end up an essential symbol of the Mayans because it emerge as associated with their mythology about the holy tree of existence. There is a sacred tree that symbolizes existence that the fingers at the pass stand for. The tree's vertical axis is the link a number of the 3 worlds. There is a danger that the Mayans had been more open to the float when seen on this manner, but this concept has not been demonstrated.

In Mayan folklore, the bough of life is a fairly huge discern regarding how the

Mayans saw the universe. As informed via the Mayans, the holy tree of existence started out out within the Underworld, spread via the arena of the dwelling, after which rose to the heavens. Earth were given life from it in the direction of its rise, and it later set the heavens, collectively with unique celestial matters, in movement. In this way, the Mayans determined the tree life as a instantly line that connected all 3 cosmos spheres. The Mayans belief the ceiba tree's shape represented the holy tree of life inside the real international. Ceiba timber were grown in Mayan cities and although are within the middle of Mayan villages due to this.

Some people assume that the Mayans have been greater open to the Christian bypass as a spiritual signal after Spain conquered them as it regarded like a tree. Even even though this concept makes sense, it isn't always supported thru proof.

The Eerie Cart of San Pascual

In Tuxtla Gutierrez, an antique cart grinding may be heard within the streets at night. People within the vicinity recognize that this weird track is popping out of the San Pascual cart, which has been despatched to assist human beings who've exceeded away pass over to wherein they'll stay forever. People say that the horrifying cart actions thru the pitch-black streets at the same time as being pushed with the aid of the usage of a skeleton monk. It starts at the cathedral of San Pascualito, wherein the statue of San Pascual is stored. The cart in the long run stops on the house wherein a person is loss of life. The cart is going away right away because the individual dies.

People close to a affected person pray for a saint however do no longer prevent at their house due to the truth the sound of the antique cart grinding hurts them. Few human beings are brave enough to appearance out of their domestic home windows, but most say now not to because they may see the cart and the spirit saint. People suppose that if the skeleton monk seems at someone, his spirit receives at the cart while his frame stays however. Scared people go with the drift a long way from their home home windows and flip off any closing lighting interior their houses People who're curious and look except pray that the ghostly saint ought to no longer see them. When the cart is heard going through the usage of, a bone-chilling wind comes through the houses and makes matters even worse. Even despite the fact that human beings try and cowl from San Pascual and his buying cart, they seize all of us.